HAGS, HAINTS, & HOODOO
A Supernatural Short Story Collection

By
Violette L. Meier

Viori Publishing

Viori Publishing
Decatur, GA

Copyright ©2020 by Violette L. Meier

ISBN: 978-0-9913432-7-0

Printed in the United States of America

Cover Art by Violette L. Meier
Cover Designed by Viori Publishing

DEDICATED

…to all who love to laugh at the things that go bump in the night.

…my family, friends, and fans. You're the absolute greatest in creation!

…God. Thank you for all things.

OTHER BOOKS BY VIOLETTE L. MEIER

PROSE
Out of Night: The First Chronicle of Zayashariya

Angel Crush

Son of the Rock
(Sequel to Angel Crush)

Archfiend
(Part 3 of the *Angel Crush* saga)

Ruah the Immortal

Tales of a Numinous Nature: A Short Story Collection

POETRY
Violette Ardor: A Volume of Poetry

*This Sickness We Call Love: Poems of Love, Lust, &
Lamentation*

INSPIRATION
Living and Loving Life One Day at a Time

CHILDREN'S BOOKS
I Would Love You

Would You Love Me?

HAGS, HAINTS, & HOODOO
A Supernatural Short Story Collection

By
Violette L. Meier

TABLE OF CONTENTS

After the Sky Fell   7

Another Day in the A   13

Bluebeard   24

Do You Believe in Magic?   44

Oddballs   51

Peaches   67

Pickles by the River   82

Reminiscing   103

Samson and Delilah   118

School Bus Stop   130

Serket   137

Wedding Day Karma   147

AFTER THE SKY FELL

Seven-year-old Sheebah used to be afraid, but now she was just lonely. She had been quarantined for what must have been a month. White suits passed her door constantly. Periodically they would come and stand outside the bubble where she was kept and whispered to each other as they wrote on clipboards stuffed with paper. They were covered from top to bottom in white suits with tubes spaghetti-ing around the back of their heads. Mirrored visors in the front of their head pieces reflected Sheebah's own small face and her metallic gold bodysuit.

She had no idea who they were or how she got there. Sheebah was very confused about why they were keeping her. She wanted to go home, but she knew that her family was gone. All of them perished when burning rocks rained from the sky like flaming mountains. She remembered the event vividly.

Sheebah and her family were playing double-dutch in the park when the sky began to fall. It was Sheebah's turn to jump into the spinning ropes. Rocking back and forth trying to catch the rhythm, the beads in her hair swaying and making music in her ears, when her cousin dropped the jump ropes and pointed to the sky. The heavens turned from cerulean to violet to pitch black and scarlet. People ran aimlessly. Screams echoed through the air like wailing sirens. Mothers gathered their children like hens guarding their chicks under their wings. Fathers grabbed the hands of their terrified children and tossed them under makeshift shelters. The ground quaked as tongues of fire leapt from the earth every time a gigantic falling object hit the ground. People were thrown off of their feet, crushed under space matter, and burned to smithereens. Sheebah stood and watched, unaffected and staring in wonder as the world ended around her. The shaking ground did not unearth her feet. The blinding light did not dim her eyes. The infernal heat did not singe her wooly hair, nor did it warm her skin, a matter of fact, it only made her onyx skin glisten in the fire light, accentuating her natural beauty as if her melanin absorbed the blaze making her luminescent.

When the fire from heaven stopped falling, Sheebah stood surrounded by tattered flesh and splattered blood. She cried out for her family but could not decipher one torn limb from another. She stood alone amidst the gory death garden in awe of the total destruction; metal and plastic from the playground married flesh and earth in jagged pieces of muck. Nothing resembled its original state. Only Sheebah was unscathed.

A white suit leaned in to observe Sheebah closer; then, scribbled something on its clipboard. Three more white suits came to her bubble and leaned in towards her, their mirrors tilting to the side. One of the suits began to unzip Sheebah's bubble. Once open, the white suit held its hand out to Sheebah. She reluctantly reached out but did accept because she wanted to be free from her plastic prison.

"Hi," Sheebah whispered, her fingers fidgeting and feet shuffling. She looked into the suit's mirror and wondered who was behind it.

The suit nodded its head. It hit a button on the front of its suit and a recording of Sheebah's voice played then morphed into a different language. The suit said something then it was translated as, "Hello. Nice to meet you."

The suit walked Sheebah over to an oval table and sat some edibles in front of her. She ate greedily. This was the first time that she had eaten since the day the sky fell. While in captivity, they put her through a strange machine, daily, which filled her belly and released her waste without requiring eating or using the bathroom. The machine was painless, but Sheebah missed the taste of food and the privacy of digestive flux. She decimated the food, which was surprisingly tasty;

it reminded her of Memphis barbeque and mango coleslaw; then, sucked up a packet of water.

Sheebah looked at the suit and asked, "When can I go home?"

The suit said, "Your people were destroyed in the takeover. Somehow you survived. We brought you with us because you are obviously a powerful being."

Sheebah's lips bent downward with the realization that she would probably be alone forever.

The suit reached out and patted Sheebah's shoulder and said, "If you want, you can stay with us. Would you like that? We will take good care of you."

Sheebah thought about it for a minute. There were no options, so she nodded her head; then, hugged the white suit.

The suit laughed and said, "Let me take this off. We now know that you are not a potential threat to our immune system."

Sheebah smiled with excitement. She was ready to meet her new friend. Sheebah imagined the person in the suit would look like her grandma Ethel with blue hair and a slight mustache. Grandma Ethel was the most beautiful woman in the world. Sheebah wondered if her grandmother had escaped the firestorm. Tears streamed from her eyes at the thought of her grandmother blown to pieces like the others.

"Here, here child," the suit wiped Sheebah's tears away. "Everything will work out fine. You will see."

The suit reached above its head and began to unzip the giant white suit. It dropped to the floor like a banana peel. Sheebah's eyes became wide as saucers as they lay upon the giant serpentine creature standing before her. It reached out its scaly olive-green hand and said, "I'm Wadjet, the protector of kings and queens, Ancestor of the Dogons, servant of Nummo and Nommo."

Wadjet curtsied, turned and gestured to another white suit. The suit left the room and came back a few minutes later escorting a young light brown boy around the age of ten wearing a metallic gold suit like Sheebah's. Next to him was a girl and a boy who looked identical to him and Sheebah, perfect twins.

"Meet Solomon sweet Sheebah, and your other self," Wadjet introduced. "Through all of you, humanity will survive. We have cleansed the earth. All pollution, evil, war, and injustice is gone. The future is yours!"

The serpent creature bowed down before Solomon and Sheebah and their doppelgangers.

Every white suit unzipped to reveal the serpentine creatures within them. The alien race prostrated in unison as the four children looked bravely at each other full of confusion, curiosity and wonder.

ANOTHER DAY IN THE A

I used to hate my life. People assume that all black folks in Atlanta love their lives; like migrating here came with a bag of fairy dust, a money tree, and a genie with unlimited wishes. I really used to really hate my life. I was not living the dream. Everything was so freaking blah until I met *him*. He changed my perspective on it all. Now, I live everyday like it is my last. I know some women are rolling their eyes saying to themselves, "Why she gotta get saved by a man? Save yourself!" This is not that kind of story, so relax. There will be no knights in shining armor, and no one is riding off on a white horse. I guess it is better to say that he helped me change my perspective. Because of him, I've learned to love hard and live free! Carpe Diem is my motto and I am happier for it. Why am I so ecstatic you ask? Allow me to explain.

I am not new to Atlanta. I was born here. Living in Atlanta and being from Atlanta is like being a unicorn. Native Atlantans are indeed a rare breed. I grew up on Patterson Avenue near where Memorial Drive crosses Moreland Avenue in East Atlanta; not too far from Kirkwood or Little Five Points. My neighborhood was old and full of great old people. Everyone knew everyone and everyone looked out for everyone. My Uncle Cyrus walked me home from school every day before he went back up the street to sit on the wall across the street from the liquor store and drank himself unconscious. Once I found him lying in Mr. Moore's yard, and I ran home screaming because I thought death had taken him. Fortunately, it was just Colt 45. My grandfather and my Uncle Willie had to carry him home as I walked behind them in a trail of tears.

By the time I was in middle school, I walked myself to school and I became immune to my uncle's harmless drunkenness, the root worker and her gang of hounds, people arguing with street poles, and overaged boys who waved for me to follow them into their homes with candy in one hand and the other hand on their crotches. I learned to ignore and ignore I did. Living in the city of Atlanta one had to learn to ignore many things.

By high school, I moved to Dekalb County where I discovered it was greater in Decatur. I was popular in high school and realized that I was piping hot. At first, I was not aware of this. I was very unconscious of my physical. I was more interested in fashion and poetry. I was made aware that I was fine by mean upper-class girls and nice upper-class boys. I never did rediscover the meaning of humility. There was no need. If you got it, flaunt it, and I .

Soon, it was back to Atlanta for college. I got my education in the middle of the AUC (Atlanta University Center). There is no greater education for a black person than one from an HBCU. College was full of exploration, lust, and learning. Freak-Nik stole my innocence and someone stole my identity when I lost my purse during registration. I partied myself onto academic probation but redeemed myself until I graduated Cum Laude. Honesty, it was thank ya Lordy, but the first sounds better. When I finally graduated, I moved into a one-bedroom apartment off Peachtree Street near the Fox Theater. There, I hobbled in and out of my apartment everyday like a lifeless zombie. I worked, ate, slept, and did it all over again day after day. I worked as a program director for a nonprofit organization whom I did not believe in nor did they seem to believe in me. I hated my life. I hated my life because I had no life. I had no man, no fun, no real friends, nothing! My life sucked and frankly I was tired of living it. Every day was a mindless hustle to support a life I wasn't fully living. I couldn't remember the last time I painted, wrote a poem, or danced. I didn't do anything I loved doing anymore and I couldn't understand what was stopping me. I guess complaining and misery became comfortable.

When the first hot summer day came that year, I decided to accept an invite to a swanky "all white" pool party. I squeezed my big bootie in the slinkiest white bikini I could find, pulled my gigantic afro into a puff ball, put on some diamond hoop earrings, four-inch heels, grabbed my bag and made my way to the party. My life sucked, but at least I was cute. The mirror was always kind; the only thing that was ever kind.

The house was ginormous and right smack in the middle of Buckhead. I pulled through the gated driveway and watched as the gate closed slowly behind me. Trees hid the house from the street, hiding the mammoth mansion from outside viewers. A valet took my car, and I made my way through the house to the pool out back.

Glistening black bodies dipped in and out of the water as laughter floated through the air. I sat on a pool chair posing like I had a personal photographer. My friend Princess (She gave herself that name. By the way- her real name was Noreeva) sat next to me chattering nonstop about some weird bearded dude sitting across from us staring at me like a piece of steak. He was hot but something about him was unnerving, so I rolled my eyes, tuned her out, and laid back to let the hot sun turn my yellow skin brown.

The lower the sun got, the stronger the smell of weed became, and the more cups ran over with cocktails. I drank, flirted, and drank some more. Noreeva had long left me for a new boy toy. See, that's what I'm talking about. No real friends! I was kinda jealous. I hadn't been touched by a man in so long that I was sure that my hymen had regenerated. Not that men didn't try to holla, it's just that there was always something wrong with them like the last guy who walked over to introduce himself. He was very handsome but one of his ears were noticeably smaller than the other. I cut the conversation short. Noreeva told me I was being extra. I rolled my eyes and took another sip. It didn't matter. The party sucked like everything else had sucked lately so I decided to go home. I stood up, one butt cheek completely hanging out of my bikini bottom, my ankles twisting in my heels because I was way too tipsy for balance, but I made my way to the valet anyway. An odd-looking pink man hesitantly handed me my car keys after I yelled at him twice to hand them over. He shook his head and walked away after he saw me swerve down the driveway.

I turned down Peachtree and drove towards home, my car struggling to stay in its lane.

I prayed that the APD was somewhere harassing some "up and coming" rapper. Lord knows there was one of them on every block. I passed Amtrak, SCAD, The High Museum, and soon the sign for The Fox came into view. I was home. My car pulled into my lot as I fumbled to find my parking pass. I let myself in after dropping the pass several times on the car floor. At an angle, my car swerved into two parking spaces and stopped. I opened my door and spilled out like the two cocktails I drank. Oh, I forgot to mention that I am not a drinker. A matter of fact, I had never drunk alcohol before that night. I mean none. Not a sip! I figured my life wasn't happy sober so I might as well try it drunk.

Every eye was on me as I shuffled down the hallway with my bikini wedgie, which looked like a thong by now, hardly putting one foot in front of the other. I somehow made the wrong turn and walked into the workout room. It was empty, dark, and surprisingly unlocked considering it was supposed to be closed at 11:30pm and it was 3:12 in the morning. I stumbled forward and lost my footing. My butt hit the floor hard. I was too drunk to cry. I grabbed hold to the end of a barbell and tried to pull myself up but my ankle twisted and the side of my head slammed into the end of the barbell. Everything went black.

When I woke up, I was sober and there *he* was. He was sitting on the bench next to the barbell that had laid me out. Tall, dark, slender but muscular with a shiny beard and mysterious eyes; kinda sexy. He could get it. I looked down at his feet and there I was lying in a pool of scarlet liquid. I blinked and looked again. I was confused. How could I be standing and looking eye to eye with him and simultaneously be on the floor?

"Velvet," he said. "Finally, nice to meet you." He pulled a fat cigar from his pocket and crossed his legs. He was dressed in a polo style shirt, a crisp pair of jeans, and a wristwatch that seemed to sparkle with an eerie sheen.

"Who are you?" I asked. I wouldn't say I was scared but seeing my body at his feet was a bit disconcerting.

"You know me," he answered taking a puff; his watch glowing in the smoke like a lighthouse in the night.

"No, I don't!" I snapped, but something in me knew who he was. My soul recognized him.

"You ready?" he asked.

"Ready for what?" I stammered nervously as I locked and unlocked my fingers. My eyes darted between his eyes and my body. He sat there quietly smoking, waiting for me to make up my mind.

"You know what," he answered looking at his watch. "Time is precious. Make up your mind."

I looked into his eyes, then back at my unconscious body sprawled at his feet. My stomach thundered. If a spirit or whatever the heck I was, could sweat, that is what I was doing, and I was doing it hard.

"Life sucks. Right?" he said between puffs, his brown eyes piercing and captivating.

I looked down at my body and went into a mental panic. For some reason, it wasn't until his words that I realized that I was actually dead. Seeing my body on the floor didn't even drive home that fact. It was his question. His eyes. His watch that made me realize that I was out of time.

"No!" I squealed. "I love my life!" Tears streamed down my face. My feet moved from side to side as I squeezed my hands together. Thoughts of my parents, siblings, and friends flooded my mind. Memories of girl trips, graduations, first love, college sweethearts, and job promotions danced around in my head. Hopes of getting married, seeing the world, having children, growing old bubbled up in my chest.

"I have a family who loves me and a good job. I have my own apartment and a little money in the bank," I blubbered, snot running into my mouth.

"Interesting," he said, a slight smile on his face. "You said your life sucked."

"I know I can be a little ungrateful, and disinterested, and bored, and dissatisfied with everything, but I love my life! I do. I really do!" I cried seeing my body cold and unmoving near the tip of his expensive sneakers. Every time he looked at his watch, I felt like all hope was gone. "I have so many things to do and places to go. I still have three hundred and twenty-five things to cross off my bucket list."

He stood up and I thought I would crap myself. He moved towards me. I wanted to step backwards but could not move my legs. I wasn't even sure that I still had legs. Maybe the bottom half of my body was a whiff of smoke or something. I looked down and there they were. I breathed a sigh of relief, but that was short lived when I found myself almost nose to nose with this strange man.

"Now you wanna live?" he asked almost rhetorically, as if he was scoffing at my back peddling.

"Yes," I whimpered.

"How bad you want it?" he smirked a smirk that made my stomach flip in a way that I could not decide if it was good or bad.

"Real bad," I whispered.

He stepped closer and grabbed the back of my head. I thought I would die again. His lips touched mine. He parted my mouth with is tongue and kissed me so deeply and completely I almost considered staying dead if this is what heaven felt like. His lips were soft, but his kiss firm. I felt it all over my body. The kiss lasted what felt like seven days and seven nights.

"Then live," he whispered into my mouth, his dark hands holding the sides of my face.

I swallowed his breath like spun sugar. He pulled back and was gone; faded into the air like his cigar smoke. Only the smell of his cologne lingered. I fell to the floor, merging with myself. I sat up holding my bloody head. I looked around the empty, dark workout room. There was no one there but me. After I managed to take my shoes off, I pulled myself to my feet and stumbled into the hallway. Using the wall as a support, I made my way to the reception desk and fainted. When my eyes opened again, I was staring up into the green eyes of a nurse. I looked down at my wrist at a band that read "Grady Memorial Hospital" along with my name: Velvet Covingtree. I shook my head. I knew I was going to be there all night.

"Hey there. Are you okay?" she asked, cleaning my wound.

I nodded; my eyes trying to focus on her face which was stern but kind.

"You have quite a cut, but the wound has been stitched and the scarring should be minimal. What happened?" she asked while writing on a clipboard.

"Another day in the A," I responded with a crooked smile. "You wouldn't believe me if I told you."

BLUE BEARD

Izan Bluebeard was a fine-looking man; tall and coffee colored with a thick shiny beard so black that it looked blue. A dazzling smile complimented his dark gypsy eyes which lured most women at first glance; yet with all his attractiveness and charisma, he couldn't seem to keep the women he wooed. He was a charming man with a cruel edge that made women love and hate him simultaneously, which may explain why he was a young man of forty in pursuit of his ninth wife.

Bluebeard lived in the tallest skyscraper overlooking the city of Atlanta. Luxury and affluence were his closest companions. There was very little that his money could not buy, and ironically very little he wanted to buy. That's why it annoyed him to no end that the woman on the other end of his phone refused to sell him her home.

The house was a small house in east Atlanta that drew him in the moment he saw it. The neighborhood was amid gentrification which explained new houses sprinkled between old ones. The house wasn't especially unique. A matter of fact, it was the opposite. It was a white frame house with a closed in porch. The front yard was small opposed to the large uneven backyard.

There was nothing visually stimulating about the home, but there was an energy that exuded from it that made his skin tickle every time he saw it.

"Name your price and I will pay you double," Bluebeard coaxed as he sat on a pillow-free couch in front of a half-wall sized television. Raven dreadlocks were tied into a neat ponytail that hung down his shirtless back. He crossed his legs and tapped his fingers impatiently on the arm of a crimson sofa.

"My home is not for sale," the woman said. "This was my great grandmother's house and it was important to her that the house remains in the family. How did you get my phone number?"

"I have my ways," Bluebeard grumbled as his thumping fingers balled into a fist. "Maybe your husband will be more reasonable."

"I have no husband," she snapped. "Thanks for the offer, but I respectfully decline. Please do not call me again," she said disconnecting the call.

Bluebeard looked at his cell phone with utter shock on his face. Never had anyone hung up on him before. He laughed. He had to meet this woman face to face. Tomorrow would be as good a time as any.

It was eighty-five degrees outside, but the humidity made it feel like one hundred. Izan

Bluebeard sat in the back of a black Mercedes-Benz parked in front of the little white house and watched patiently for someone to exit. His driver played puzzle games on his cell phone as Bluebeard watched the door with eagle eyes. Two hours passed before Bluebeard spotted a slim brown woman walking up the street wearing skinny jeans and a tank top that read, *It's not that serious.* A thick afro was pulled to the side of her head like a giant black cotton ball. Kind eyes shined from a pretty angular face. She paused and looked into the window of the car parked in front of her home.

Bluebeard opened the car door and stepped onto the sidewalk. He extended his hand to the woman; she looked at it then crossed her arms. He smiled mischievously. She frowned completely unimpressed.

"How may I help you?" she asked, the kindness in her eyes turning into something a lot more serious.

Bluebeard extended his hand again and said, "I'm Izan Bluebeard. I called you yesterday about your house."

"Didn't I make it clear that I was not interested in your proposal? You are making me really uncomfortable," she said as she pulled her cell phone from her back pocket readying herself to call the police.

"Wait," Bluebeard implored. "Let's start over. I respect your decision not to sell the house. I just want to ask you about the history of it."

The woman's face softened. She put her phone back into her pocket and crossed her arms again.

"Why?" she asked; sparkling lip gloss making her lips twinkle like a thousand stars.

"Your home intrigues me. I heard that your great grandmother was a very respected woman. I am very sorry to hear about her passing. I read an article about her in the local paper. Her love of family and community was inspiring," he answered.

"Yes, she was. She was a wise woman with the gift of interpreting dreams. Some say she was a natural witch. Make no mistake, she did not practice the occult. She just knew things, like how to bend the elements around her. We were very close. Grandma was a very interesting woman," the woman said dropping her arms and extending her hand. "My name is Aminah Thomas. Nice to meet you."

Bluebeard shook her hand.

"I'm sure you miss her a lot," he said letting the handshake linger.

"Believe it or not, her death hasn't set in yet. It has been over six months and I still feel her all around me," Aminah admitted. "That's why the house is so important to me. I can feel my grandmother there." She paused. "Funny story; one night I was awakened by a noise. I thought I heard someone outside of my window. Then, I thought I heard my great grandmother shooing them away. When I got up to look, my window lock was broken and there was a tennis shoe in my front yard as if someone ran away so fast that their shoe fell off and they just left it behind."

Bluebeard raised an eyebrow. He didn't believe in such things, but she was attractive, and he wanted that house, so he decided to entertain it.

"May I take you for coffee?" he asked. "I would love to hear more. I am heavily into genealogy. I can trace my mother's side to Nigeria and my father's side to France, hence the name Bluebeard." He bowed. "Maybe I can help you learn more about your lineage."

Aminah laughed. For the first time she noticed how handsome and well-made he looked in his fitted designer suit. Suddenly she felt underdressed. She contemplated trading her jeans for a sundress and letting her hair down, but she didn't want to give the wrong impression.

"I don't drink coffee, but there is a juice bar up the street. I will meet you there in fifteen minutes," she said as she opened her screen door and came back down the walkway with a ten-speed bike. "Make a right at the end of the street and a left at the intersection. It is the purple building on the corner."

"I have room in my car," Bluebeard grinned.

Aminah jumped on her bike and headed down the hill before he could settle into the backseat.

Talk over juice turned into light lunches and romantic dinners. Days turned into weeks and weeks turned into months. On their seventh month of dating, Izan Bluebeard decided that he would make Aminah Thomas his ninth wife. That way he would have access to the house that he had been coveting; the house that Aminah had refused to let him step foot in.

"You look so freaking beautiful," Bluebeard whispered into Aminah's ear and gave her a soft kiss on the neck. He stepped back to take in the form fitting dress that hugged her in all the right places. Her afro was pinned into a French roll decorated with violets; her lips were fire engine red.

"Thank you," she said bashfully.

"Where are we going tonight?" Aminah asked.

"It's a surprise," he answered and ushered her into the car.

In about a half an hour, they pulled up to a park. White lights decorated the trees. The couple walked down a path made of rose pedals to a candle lit table. Aminah forced a smile. The sentiment was sweet but a bit Hollywood. She was a simple woman who would have been happier if they walked barefoot in the grass feeding each other mango slices.

"How sweet Izan," she grinned. "All this for me?"

"And more," Bluebeard replied with a wave of his hand. A trio of violinists stepped out of the trees and began playing her favorite Prince song. At this, she genuinely grinned.

After dinner, the two went back to his penthouse. It was her first time inside. As a rule, she refused to enter a man's house that she was not sleeping with. Tonight, seemed like a perfect night to change that. It was time to take things to the next level.

He placed his hand upon a small computer screen next to his front door.

"What's that?" she asked.

"The key," he answered taking her hand and scanning the prints onto the screen. "Now my home is your home. You may enter anytime just by putting your palm to the screen. All I ask is that you do not use it to enter my wine cellar. It is a sacred place for me. Something of a man cave. Okay?"

"Okay," she agreed as they walked into the apartment.

Aminah was floored by the massive space, original paintings on the wall, hardwood floors, and tasteful furniture. It was simply beautiful.

"Would you like something to drink?" Bluebeard asked as he dropped his keys on the counter and tossed his suit jacket over the back of a chair.

"No thank you," Aminah said as she put her purse on a table and walked over to him. She wrapped her arms around his neck and gave him a long, deep kiss. "Thank you so much for a beautiful night. You made me feel loved."

Bluebeard smiled. He had never told her that he loved her. He knew that is what she wanted to hear, but to say such things were not in his nature.

"I'm glad," he responded touching her chin and putting his other hand in his pocket. He pulled out a ring box and dropped down on one knee.

"I want you to always feel that way," said Bluebeard. "Will you be my wife?"

Aminah hesitated. Words abandoned her. She liked him a lot, but she wasn't sure if she could marry someone who obviously didn't take marriage seriously. If she accepted, she would be his ninth wife. But, on the other hand, maybe his relationships were not that bad because he had zero problems from his exes. She had to admit, the idea of marrying a rich man was alluring. She was knee-high in student loan debt, needed seed money for a business, and was living from paycheck to paycheck. Money was a huge stressor for her, but she tried to hold close to what her great grandmother told her before she died. The old woman had a dream that Aminah would come into a large sum of money and prime real estate. Aminah didn't know how that was going to happen considering the fact that she only earned $30,000 a year and the only real estate she owned was gifted to her by her great grandmother. Maybe marrying Bluebeard would be the source of her wealth.

"Will you?" Bluebeard asked, his brow beginning to furrow and his eyes getting darker by the moment. Rejection was not an option.

"Look, I care about you a lot. This is all moving so fast. Let me think about it," Aminah said. She kissed his forehead and then his eyelids. Aminah wanted to marry for love, not money; besides, there was something sinister behind his eyes that she could not put her finger on, and his overly aggressive personality made her weary at times.

"To prove to you that my love is sincere, I have taken out a life insurance policy on myself and made you the beneficiary. I have also left everything that I own to you in my will," he said pointing to an envelope hanging from his jacket pocket.

Aminah felt strange inside. It was odd to speak about death before starting a new life. She forced a smile and tried to hide the discomfort in her eyes.

"Later this week, I will arrange for you to do the same for me," Bluebeard stated.

"Let's make tonight wonderful. It is not time for such serious talk," she said to change the subject. There was no way in the world that she was going to write him into her will or allow him to get a life insurance policy on her.

Bluebeard got up from the floor and led her into the bedroom where his anger was revealed by every savage stroke, hard slap, and random hair pull. He was rough, unmerciful, and sadistic. After a turbulent night of frightening passion, Aminah knew that he was not the one for her. She had no intention of ever letting him put his hands on her again.

"Wake up!" Bluebeard shouted.

Aminah sat up in bed and Bluebeard placed a tray of food on her lap. She ate slowly. Her whole body ached. She was sure that bruises freckled her body everywhere.

"I have to take a day trip for work. Stay here and get comfortable. This will be your home soon," he said, packing his bag and slipping his feet into his shoes. "Feel free to invite friends over or just curl up on the couch. Remember my wine closet is off limits."

"I think I'll just go home," she responded as she tried to throw her legs over the side of the bed, but they hurt too much to move.

"Take time to recover. My guard is outside the door and he will get you anything you need. Relax. I will be back tomorrow." He laughed, "You were a handful last night."

She shot him an angry glance.

"We need to talk about that," she hissed.

"No need. I know you are a bit uncomfortable, but you will get used to it." He kissed her forehead and walked out of the room.

Aminah heard the front door close and she dropped off the side of the bed. She crawled into the bathroom and pulled herself onto the toilet. It took all the balance she could muster to lean over and turn on the tub water. Steam filled the bathroom quickly. When the water was high enough, she climbed in and allowed the hot water to sooth her pain. Within seconds, her eyes were closed, and she was transported into the land of dreams.

He is not for you. A voice whispered in her ear. *Get out now or you will become one of us!* Aminah's eyes popped open. There was no one there. She turned on the hot water to raise the temperature of the water then closed her eyes. *Go now or never!* Another voice spat. Aminah sat up in the tub and searched the room with her eyes. She pulled the drain, stood up, grabbed a towel, and wrapped it around her. *Get out!* Aminah ran out of the bathroom into the bedroom where she saw the TV on. She let out a sigh of relief. It must have been the TV.

Aminah pulled a t-shirt out of Bluebeard's drawer and put it on. It hung down to her thighs making her look like a small child. She sat on the side of the bed until she could not hold in her curiosity any longer. Aminah rambled through his drawers, closet, medicine cabinet and nightstands.

There were old pictures of women she assumed were his ex-wives. All of them were as different as right was from left. They were all ethnicities, different body types, and heights. They only thing they had in common was their extreme beauty. Aminah felt flattered to be among such beautiful women.

She walked out of the bedroom into the hallway. There were two guest rooms, an office, and another bathroom. Each room was decorated exquisitely; complete with fine art, unique furniture, and state of the art entertainment systems. A door with a computer screen on it was located at the far end of the hallway. She approached it.

"This must be the wine cellar," she uttered. "What is he hiding?"

Aminah paced back and forth in front of the door.

"I've already violated the man's privacy. I can't just do exactly what he asked me not to do," she argued with herself. "But, I need to know what he's into; if things can get worse than last night. What if I decide to say I do in the distant future?"

Aminah slapped her hand against the screen and the door slid open. She walked inside. It was dark. She felt around on the walls for a switch. There was not one, but she felt the necks of wine bottles. She kept walking until another computer screen glowed on the front of an iron door. Aminah touched the screen and the metal door opened. A terrible smell hit Aminah's nose. A thick, wet darkness surrounded her. She searched for a light switch as she walked. Something mushy squished between her toes. Her skin crawled. Aminah damned herself for not bringing her cell phone. Her fingers ran across the wall until she felt a button. She pushed it. A dim light blinked and grew stronger. Aminah's eyes stretched wide as she saw the mutilated bodies of eight women hanging on hooks dangling from the ceiling. A bloody head turned to her, its eyes gashed out and teeth missing. It screamed, "Get out!"

Aminah vomited on her own feet, then kicked away the liquid and turned and ran from the room, her feet tracking mushy human parts and vomit down the hall. She ran into the main apartment and closed the wine closet door behind her. She rushed into the bedroom and dressed frantically; then, ran into the kitchen and grabbed a mop and cleaner. She mopped the hallway floor and placed the cleaning products back in their place. Aminah gathered her things and opened the front door.

A big pink skinned man with a bald head turned around and asked, "How may I help you Miss Aminah?"

"I'm going home. Will you drive me?" she asked, her voice cracking and her hands trembling uncontrollably.

"Are you okay?" he asked.

"I think I have the stomach flu. I rather be in my own bed," Aminah lied.

"Mr. Bluebeard insisted that you stay here," the guard said.

"I'm leaving. You...you...you can drive me, or I can call a car," Aminah stuttered.

"Okay Miss Aminah. I'm sure he will understand," the guard said as he escorted her down the hall and into an elevator. They exited the building and he took her home.

Once inside her home, Aminah could not lock all the doors fast enough. She paced the floor trying to figure out her next move. She had already decided to send an anonymous tip to the police, but how was she going to break up with him without him knowing what she discovered?

Her cell phone rang. It was him. She hit ignore, but he called back again.

"Hello," Aminah answered, her voice wavering like a criminal at trial.

"Hi sweetheart. Where are you? I came back early to surprise you and you surprised me by not being here," he asked, his voiced laced with irritation. "I thought I told you to stay put."

"I didn't feel well. I wanted to sleep in my own bed," she answered faking a cough.

"I'll bring you some soup," Bluebeard offered.

"Please don't bother. I don't have much of an appetite and I would not dream of getting you sick," whined Aminah in a high-pitched voice. Her heartbeat was so violent that she clutched her breast.

"Nonsense! My immune system is incredible. I'll be over shortly," he insisted and disconnected.

Aminah dropped her phone and began to weep.

Bluebeard walked into his kitchen and began to pack a get-well basket for his girlfriend. Soup, crackers, juice, and teas filled the small basket quickly. He grabbed his keys and stepped into the hallway. Something on the floor caught his eye. It was a faint crimson smear on his pristine white tile. Bluebeard followed the smear to the end of the hall where it stopped in front of his wine cellar. He pressed his palm into the computer screen and unlocked the door. As soon as the door opened, he saw that the door where his dead wives rested was open as well. A fierce growl rumbled from his throat. He turned on his heels and headed to Aminah's house.

A heavy knock on the door startled Aminah from the fetal position she had taken on the couch. Her feet dropped to the floor as if her bones were made of lead. She stood up and shuffled over to the door. Tears blurred her vision as she peeked through the peep hole. It was him. Aminah damned herself for opening the door the minute he stepped over the threshold.

"How are you feeling," Bluebeard asked, his words cold and forceful. He dropped the get-well package that he had made for her on the coffee table.

"Not great," her voice trembled. "Honestly, I am not feeling up to having company."

He reached to embrace her, but she recoiled from him as if his palms were made of fire.

Bluebeard stepped away from her and walked around the small living room admiring the quaintness of the house. It was the first time that he had stepped foot inside. The strange energy that he felt from the home seemed magnified.

"This is a beautiful place," he complimented. "Why haven't you invited me sooner?" he asked while walking from the living room into a large square hallway.

"Pl...pl...please don't walk through my home," Aminah stammered. "I...I...I have not finished my weekly cleaning."

He walked on as if she said nothing.

"Please!" Aminah begged. "Come back up front so that we can talk."

He walked on, going from room to room, opening and closing doors, sizing up closet space, peering through windows, and opening top drawers.

"What are you doing?" Aminah hissed; following behind him. "Please stop! You are invading my privacy!"

He turned to her and grabbed her by the neck and squeezed. He spat through his teeth, "Like you invaded mine!"

Aminah clawed at his face until he dropped her to the floor. She leapt up and ran into the living room to get her cell phone. He was right on her heels. Bluebeard grabbed her hair and she grabbed a lamp and hit him across the face with it. He stumbled backwards holding his eye; a slew of curse words permeated the room. Aminah grabbed her phone, but before she could dial 911,

Bluebeard was on top of her, his hand tight around her neck again and her head pushed deep into the sofa pillows. Muffled screams faded into the couch as she flailed fruitlessly.

Bluebeard cackled, "I hate that it has to end this way. If you would have sold me the house from the beginning, I would not have had to waste all these months pretending to like you. Now you will have to join those other nosey heifers I had to put to sleep. I'm going to have the best time torturing you! When you wake up, you will be hanging from the highest hook with a thorny muzzle covering your big mouth!"

Aminah kicked and kicked, but his weight on her back only made things harder. Everything was becoming black. Sounds of his laughing faded into a soft voice that sounded familiar.

Bluebeard pushed the back of Aminah's head down with both of his hands when someone grabbed the back of his neck and threw him to the floor as if he was as light as a feather. A tall gray-haired woman stood over him with destruction in her eyes. He tried to get to his feet, but she raised her hands above her head and chanted something indecipherable. A faint glow covered him from head to toe. In complete horror, he watched the faint light engulf him. His insides felt like he had swallowed flames. In a manner of seconds, Bluebeard had become a pile of ashes.

The old woman went over to Aminah, lifted her unconscious body, and cradled her in her arms. She kissed Aminah's forehead and the young woman opened her eyes.

"Grandma," Aminah whispered. "I knew you were here."

"Always," the old woman uttered and faded away dropping Aminah softly onto the sofa. Aminah pulled herself to her feet and gathered a broom, dustpan, and trash can from the kitchen. She swept up Bluebeard's ashes and took them to her backyard where she mixed them in with garden soil. After cleaning herself up, she called the police station and left an anonymous tip about the dead women in Bluebeard's house.

A year later, Aminah's life had regained some sense of normalcy and Bluebeard was assumed dead, she was contacted by Bluebeard's lawyers and was given the deeds to a dozen properties and awarded a five-million-dollar life insurance policy. Tears streamed down her eyes a she remembered her grandmother's dream. Aminah whispered, "Thank you Grandma."

A small voice echoed through the house, "You're welcome."

DO YOU BELIEVE IN MAGIC?

"Do you believe in magic?" Valerie asked as she plopped down on her best friend's bed; kicking her shoes off and falling back onto the pillows. It felt so good to sit down. Her feet hurt from a long day running back and forth between meetings and her head hurt from the lingering demands of finicky clients. Although Valerie was a bit warm, she was too lazy to remove her blazer. The comfort of her feet was enough for now.

It had been a long week and she was ecstatic that the weekend had come. Social media marketing conventions, traveling to three cities and back, and meeting a last-minute deadline made Valerie so tired that she was surprised that she had made it to Latrell's house.

"Why?" Latrell laughed, her round cheeks shining in the room light. Glittering gold highlighter sparkled all over her face reminding Valerie of a disco ball. "You always ask the most random questions. I swear, you get weirder by the day." Latrell sat at a small desk in the corner of her bedroom typing on her laptop.

"Don't remind me," Valerie sighed.

It was true. Valerie had always been the odd man out. As an albino, she was the palest black girl at her elementary school which made her a target for cruel white girl and alien jokes. Her metal mouth and corrective shoes did little to help matters. By the time she was in middle school, they called her pizza face because of her neon red pimples. In high school, she was underdeveloped and skinny. They called her lonely because she had no body. By the time Valerie got into college, her body developed, she grew into her beauty, she excelled in school, but her odd mannerisms still made her an outcast to everyone except Latrell. They had been friends since their freshman year in college.

"Do you?" Valerie asked again.

"Not really. Why?" Latrell answered, turning around to face her friend. Extremely cute, Latrell had a round beige face like a chipmunk. When she smiled, pure joy exuded.

"I think I may know how to do magic," Valerie confessed, removing her jacket and fluffing the pillows behind her.

"I ain't got time for your musings. I got work to do," Latrell said, spinning back around to her laptop. The sound of her tapping fingers filled the room.

"I'm serious!" Valerie laughed.

Latrell spun back around to face her friend; Latrell's eyes rolling, and her lips twisted.

"Make a million dollars appear, then make yourself vanish from my bed!" Latrell replied slapping her thighs and pouting like a toddler.

Valerie laughed.

"I'm serious Trell. I'm not talking about ritualistic, spirit channeling magic or that crazy stuff we see on TV. I'm talking about directed intention. Sheer will so powerful that it alters the world around us," Valerie replied. She picked up the TV remote and began to flip through channels. There was nothing interesting on TV, so she turned it off and began to play a game on her cell phone. "I can do things."

"Like what?" Latrell asked, surrendering to the fact that Valerie was not going to let her finish her work until an asinine conversation about magical powers occurred. Latrell loved Valerie, but her random contemplations about the numinous world worked Latrell's nerves; especially when there was a work deadline to meet.

"It's hard to explain," said Valerie.

"You better start so I can get back to work. You got five minutes," Latrell said as she held up her cell phone and tapped the time on the screen.

Still engulfed in her phone game, Valerie replied, "Sometimes I just think something, and it'll happen. Like the other day, I was really stressed out and I had no time to eat lunch. I started thinking about my favorite restaurant and less than an hour later, my co-worker came in with exactly what I wanted. He brought it to me without me asking."

"You talking about Sergio?" Latrell asked with a smirk.

"Yes!"

"He like you fool! Of course, he would do that!" Latrell snapped.

Valerie frowned and said, "He didn't know what I like to eat. Besides, there are other things that have happened too. Yesterday, I touched a client's hand and knew exactly what she wanted down to the very detail."

"That's called discernment," Latrell snapped. "You work in marketing. Knowing what your clients want is your job."

"Whatever! Last week I craved a smoothie and when I walked into my kitchen, there was a brand-new blender. I don't own a blender!" Valerie exclaimed. She began to pace the floor like a lawyer defending her case.

"You buy so much junk, you don't know what's in your kitchen," Latrell retorted.

"How do you explain this?" Valerie pointed to a small scar on her arm.

"Explain what?"

"I burned myself on the stove. It was so bad that I could see the white meat. I cried and prayed over it and it closed up and sealed itself in a matter of minutes!"

"Umhum," Latrell replied. She was getting weary of the conversation. Valerie had the propensity to exaggerate. Latrell shook her head. All she could think about was the career changing presentation she had to finish before morning.

"I got power. I know it," Valerie declared. She sat back on the bed and picked up her phone to start a new game.

"It's funny you say that. Some east Africans, like in Tanzania and Malawi, believe that albinos have magical powers," Latrell explained, overwhelmingly bored.

Valerie's eyes lit up.

Latrell continued, "It's not a positive thing. Because of the belief that body parts of albinos possess power, they're often murdered and dismembered for use in rituals and potions to bring prosperity. Some people even dig up graves to attain body parts."

Valerie gasped in horror.

"It's terrible. I know," replied Latrell in hopes of ending the conversation and getting back to work.

"It's more than terrible. It's evil," Valerie squawked. The idea of someone killing her because of her lack of melanin horrified and enraged her.

"Yes, it is," Latrell agreed.

"Why do you always have to bring up the most tragic stories?" Valerie whined. "You're ruining my excitement."

"Do you really think you have power?" Latrell asked, arms folded. She let out an exasperated sigh.

"Don't believe me then," Valerie huffed. "Finish your funky work."

Latrell laughed aloud.

Valerie was hilarious when she was mad. Her cheeks turned red, her light-colored eyes squinted, she sighed continually. She did everything short of stumping her feet.

"Don't be mad. I believe that all people have power. We have a god-force within us," Latrell explained. "I wish I could explore this more with you, but I have to get back to work."

"Okay," Valerie sighed. She pulled on her shoes and put on her jacket. "Imma head home."

When Latrell stood up to hug her friend, her stomach growled.

"You hungry?" Valerie inquired.

"Starving," Latrell replied. "I haven't eaten all day. I'll get something after I'm done."

"What are you going to get?" Valerie asked.

Latrell knew that Valerie was procrastinating. Although loved and appreciated as a dear friend, Latrell wanted Valerie out of her house.

"Chinese," Latrell mumbled as she lightly grabbed Valerie by the arm and led her to the front door. "I'll call you tomorrow."

"Goodnight," Valerie said with a mischievous smile.

"Goodnight," Latrell replied and closed the door. She walked back into her bedroom. The sweet smell of sesame chicken greeted her nose. Her eyebrow raised. There was a takeout bag sitting on her laptop. She opened it and her favorite meal was inside complete with spring rolls and duck sauce. Her cellphone buzzed. It was a text message from Valerie. It read, "Now, do you believe in magic?"

ODDBALLS

Shontell Brownfield was an extremely odd, young woman. So odd in fact, other odd people often looked at her with a side-eye. Her looks were odd. Like Frida Kahlo, a thick unibrow sat in the middle of Shontell's forehead. Her nose was pointy and turned up. Her lips were a complete circle. Wide and wild eyes with something joyfully primal pulsating behind them highlighted her face. She was short and round with oddly muscular legs which made her the plumpest and fastest track star her school had ever had. She held seven school records in track and field.

She dressed oddly. Mix-match patterns were her thing. She had the ability to make paisley, plaid, and stripes look oddly cool. In her own right, she was a fashionista who many desired to emulate.

Her personality was odd. Her laugh, which was often too loud, was a mixture of giggling and snorting. She shared random facts at random times. Shontell always answered questions with the most improbable answers. Most people liked her but found her completely annoying at the same time. Shontell was fine with that. Comfortable in her oddity and embraced it fully, her eccentricity was not a bane, but a boon.

Just when Shontell thought she couldn't get any odder, she met Calvin Clunderdew.

An incredibly popular student, Calvin played football, basketball, and baseball and exceled in them all. He was attractive; tall, mocha colored, and physically fit. There wasn't one girl at the university that didn't pine over him. Strangely, he pined over Shontell, the one girl who no one else seemed to pine over.

One sunny afternoon, while exiting the gym after football practice, Calvin saw Shontell with earbuds in her ears, pop locking outside of the student center. He couldn't help but laugh as she danced as if no one was watching. He decided then and there that it was time for them to meet. He walked up behind her and tapped her on the shoulder. She spun around and stepped backwards as if she was flowing into her next dance move.

"Hi," he said with a big smile revealing perfectly even teeth as white as tissue.

"Hi," she replied with a half-smile half-frown and a bit confused about why she was being disturbed. It was the best part of the song. She was just getting into her groove.

"My name is Calvin," he said.

"I know who you are," she replied taking her earbuds out of her ears. "Did you know that surprising someone releases dopamine in the brain which helps with attention focus?"

"Huh?" he asked. His eyebrows rose and dropped. He shook his head. This was going to be more interesting than he imagined.

"What do you want?" Shontell asked politely while neatly wrapping her earbud cord around her finger and placing it in a small case.

"I want to talk to you," he replied. "Want to go to lunch with me?"

"That's an incomplete sentence," Shontell replied.

"Do you want to go to lunch with me?" Calvin asked correctly this time. A crooked smile curved his lips. Usually, nitpicky people got on his nerves, but not Shontell. Something about her was instantly likeable. She felt like family, but not in an inbred, creepy way. He didn't look at her like a sister, more like a significant other.

Shontell stared at him for about a minute.

Calvin waved his hand in front of her face to break her trance.

"Do you?" he asked.

"Do I what?" she asked.

"Do you want to eat lunch with me today?" he repeated in a slow distorted voice. "Earth to Shontell."

Shontell nodded slowly. No one of his caliber had ever asked her to lunch before. Usually the guys that asked her to lunch laughed like donkeys and wore glasses way too big.

"Come on," Calvin said as he grabbed her hand and began to walk. She quickly matched his pace as they headed towards the parking lot. She halted and snatched her hand from his.

"Where are we going?" she asked.

"To my car," he replied. "We're going to lunch. Remember?"

"Did you know that most people are assaulted by someone that they know?" she asked folding her arms and looking into his eyes like they were going to reveal some malevolent secret.

Calvin's brows furrowed. He felt a bit insulted, but he couldn't be angry with her for worrying about her safety.

"I would never assault anyone, but I never want you to feel uncomfortable. We can eat at the student center if you like," he replied.

"No. I'm in the mood for Mexican," she replied as she snatched his keys. "I'll drive just in case."

Calvin laughed aloud and led her to his car. The couple jumped into Calvin's 1966 classic car and sped to the nearest Mexican restaurant. Shontell pulled into the parking lot with a screech.

Calvin silently thanked God that the brakes were good.

"You drive like a bat out of hell!" Calvin said as he put his hand out for his keys. She dropped them in his hand and laughed a loud snorting laugh.

"You're not driving back!" he exclaimed as he got out of the passenger side and hurried around to the driver's side of the car to open the door for her.

"Thank you," Shontell said as she got out of the car. "You know I'm capable of opening my own door."

"Me opening the door for you has nothing to do with your capabilities. It has to do with my upbringing as a gentleman and the respect I have for you as a woman," he replied.

Shontell looked at him for a second then shrugged her shoulders.

"Do you like broccoli?" she asked.

"I guess," he laughed. "Why?"

"You look like the type that likes broccoli," she replied as she waited for him to open the door to the restaurant.

"What does that mean?" he asked as he followed her to a nearby table and sat down across from her.

A pretty Hispanic woman came over and poured them both a glass of water. Her dark brown skin, black hair in two braids, and high cheekbones made Calvin think of the pictures of his paternal great grandmother. She handed them menus and silverware then disappeared into the kitchen.

"Did you know that broccoli is a part of the cabbage family. It's a wild cabbage. You look like you may enjoy wild cabbage," she replied as she looked at the menu.

Calvin laughed. "You're odd," he said.

She looked up, a little embarrassed.

"In a good way," he replied flashing a smile.

She buried her face in the menu; her heart leaping a bit.

"So, tell me about yourself," Calvin asked placing his menu on the table, then placed his hand upon her menu moving it downward.

Shontell froze for a moment then opened her mouth to speak when the waitress reappeared.

"What would you like to order?" the server asked in a thick Mixtec accent. Her eye caught a small scar on Calvin's upper arm. It looked like teeth marks. She dropped her pen and pad, and nervously picked them back up.

"Nagual!" she gasped.

Calvin covered the scar with his hand.

"What did you say?" Shontell asked the waitress.

"Nice girl," the server lied trying to force her frown into a smile. She was visibly shaken. "Very pretty."

"Thanks," said Shontell, not sold on the waitress' compliment. "I'll have vegetable fajitas with extra guacamole and sour cream, and an orange juice on ice. No rice or jalapenos. Also, can you make sure that the sour cream and guacamole don't touch? Thanks," Shontell ordered and handed the waitress the menu.

"I will have crunchy tacos and a soda. Thanks," Calvin replied and handed his menu to the waitress. The waitress hurried into the kitchen. Shouting in her indigenous tongue was heard from the back of the restaurant. Seconds later, a man stuck his head out of the kitchen door to look at Calvin. The man disappeared behind the door once more and the yelling commenced.

"What's with her?" Shontell asked.

"Who knows," replied Calvin. "I think she was repulsed by my scar."

"Lemme see," Shontell asked as she grabbed his arm before he could answer.

He extended his arm to allow for a closer look.

"Amazing!" Shontell exclaimed. "I have one just like it!" She pulled her calf-length skirt up to the middle of her thigh.

Calvin felt a gush of heat flow through him. He swallowed hard as he tried intensely to focus on the matching scar instead of her firm shapely thigh.

"Wow," he whispered. "It's just like mine."

He placed his jacket over his lap and scooted closer to the table to hide his embarrassment. He didn't anticipate her legs being so curvy and lovely. Hands down, she was not a conventional beauty, but she was definitely attractive in the most potent way. Everything about her was intoxicating; her smell, her intense eyes, her intellect. There was something primal in the way she moved. He even liked her hairy arms. His mother used to say that lots of hair meant that you had rich blood.

"How did you get yours?" he asked trying hard to cool his heated blood.

"I've had it as long as I can remember. I have a faint memory of being bitten by a giant dog when I was around three," she said. "Did you know the biggest dogs in the world are Great Danes and Mastiffs? I don't think it was either one of those who bit me. The dog I remember looked more like a Siberian Husky, but it could've been a fox or a coyote. Wolves are not native to Georgia so I'm pretty sure it wasn't a wolf. It was probably a Chihuahua. Ha. Ha. You know, when you're a kid, things always seem bigger than what they are. Do you like dogs?"

The waitress placed their dishes in front of them and scurried away.

"I'm not an animal person, but if I had to pick a favorite, it probably would be a dog or maybe a pigeon," he answered before biting into his taco.

"A pigeon?" she questioned. "That's weird. Did you know that the only difference between a pigeon and a dove is the color? Also, did you know that some people eat pigeons? It's called squab."

The waitress and the man in the kitchen peeked out of the kitchen periodically; then went back inside yelling in their language.

"How do you know all this useless information?" Calvin asked as he finished his dish. He felt that they were on borrowed time. The disturbed look on the waitress and her companion's face made Calvin uncomfortable.

"I just do," she said, shrugged her shoulders, and finished her meal as well.

"How did you get yours?" she asked wiping the guacamole from her mouth.

"Like yours, mine has been here forever. Mom said I was bitten by a dog when I was a baby. They said the dog was trying to carry me away. My grandfather tried to shoot it. It ran away and disappeared into the woods," he answered.

He paid for the meal and left a generous tip despite the waitress' strange behavior.

"Let's go," he said.

"Okay," she agreed following him out of the restaurant. They jumped in the car, Calvin behind the wheel, and drove to a hiking trail near the school.

"You feel like walking off that food," he asked.

"Sure," she said. "FYI, it's creepy to take a girl to the woods on the first date. Know that I have a black belt in karate and that I'm the fastest girl in school so I can kick you in the nuts and you won't be able to catch me."

Calvin laughed. "Don't worry. I'm harmless."

"You better be," she replied as she took his hand and started on the dirt path.

The couple walked and talked like they had known each other for a lifetime. They exchanged childhood stories, hopes and dreams, worst nightmares, and most embarrassing moments. Calvin talked about his love of sports and Shontell shared random facts about the nature surrounding them. There was something about Shontell that made him feel that she really got him; that she understood him on the deepest level; that she was the Eve to his Adam. Shontell felt the same. Never did she imagine that someone could love and accept her and all her idiosyncrasies. With his love of fried hot dogs over pancakes; his admission to toenail biting; his fear of purple flowers, he was just as odd as she was, in a good way. Shontell felt that they could be perfectly odd together.

Minutes turned into hours, and the sun began to set behind them.

Calvin turned to Shontell.

"You're beautiful," he whispered. "You're the most extraordinary woman I have ever met."

"I may be a lot of things, but beautiful I am not," she corrected. "Did you know that beauty..."

"Shhh." He placed his finger on her lips. "You're beautiful to me," he said as he closed the gap between them. He leaned in and kissed her lips. She stood frozen like a popsicle. He kissed her again, she didn't reciprocate, but he could feel the shift in her body temperature. He could sense her pheromones in the air.

"Is everything okay?" he asked.

"It's getting dark," she whispered into his open mouth. Her breath tasted like peppermint.

"Oh no!" Calvin said as he noticed that the sky had begun to turn from blue to plum. The pale full moon gained brightness in the dimming sunlight. He damned himself for not paying attention to the time.

"I think we better go home," Shontell replied.

Night pounced upon them quickly. The full moon loomed over their heads like an intimidating mother. The moonlight turned their eyes into glowing reflectors.

"Where are my keys!" Calvin panicked. He searched his pockets and came up with lint.

"I need to get home," Shontell began to fret. "I don't like to be out at night!"

"Let's retrace our steps," Calvin suggested and Shontell agreed. As they walked, Calvin noticed that Shontell's arms looked hairier than before, her legs too.

"Why are your jeans moving?" Shontell asked as she witnessed the back of his pants move aimlessly like a frog caught in his underwear.

He tied his jacket around his waist with elongated fingers.

Shontell gasped. She grimaced but closed her mouth quickly. She could feel her canines piercing her bottom lip.

"What's happening to you?" Calvin questioned.

"What's happening to you!" Shontell exclaimed as she saw a bushy tail break free from the back of his jeans.

"Maybe we should split..." Calvin started but his words morphed into an ear-piercing howl. He dropped to his knees and his clothes began to peel like an orange.

Shontell backed away, but before she could take another step, her torso flung forward until she was on all fours. Paws with sharp claws replaced hands and feet. Her skirt and top split and fell to the ground like falling leaves.

Hair became fur, smiles became maws, hands became claws, screams became howls. Two wolves began to circle each other; one grey and one golden. The golden wolf licked the maw of the grey wolf, it reciprocated. They ran off into the woods.

Morning came as mornings always do. The sun lit up the cloudless periwinkle sky. Birds chirped and bugs buzzed playing a song in mother nature's symphony.

Shontell opened her eyes. She was tucked into the arms of Calvin; both completely nude, smeared with dirt, and spooning underneath an oak tree on a bed of leaves.

"Good morning weirdo," Calvin said as he kissed the top of her head.

"Good morning," she whispered unsure if she wanted to talk about last night. "Did you know that the archaic meaning of the word weird is connected to fate? It means destiny."

"Indeed, I think you're my destiny," he laughed.

"It seems so," she agreed pensively. "I was thinking about what the lady said when we were in the Mexican restaurant. It sounded like she said nagual instead of nice girl."

"What's that?" Calvin asked although he knew she was going to tell him.

"I don't know, but I'm going to find out as soon as I get to my phone," she confessed.

"Something you don't know. I can't believe it!" Calvin kidded.

Shontell bit him on his scar and growled. He let out a lazy howl. She kissed his dirt-caked nails. He flicked a dead leaf from her unibrow and pulled a blade of grass from her ear.

"We gotta get to class. Let me get you home," he said as he got up and held out his hand to help her up. She accepted it and followed him to the car while constantly watching out for possible onlookers.

Down the path they picked up what was left of their clothes and tied them around their most sacred parts. Once in the car, they rode silently and pulled into Calvin's apartment parking lot.

"You can borrow some of my clothes," he said as they exited the vehicle. "I don't want you walking around campus half-naked. It's dangerous out there; lots of wolves in sheep's clothing."

"Okay," she laughed.

Calvin opened the apartment door. Much to his dismay, one of his roommates was sitting in the living room playing a video game.

"What ya'll got on?" Calvin's roommate yelled when they walked inside of the apartment. "Ya'll went to a zombie convention or something?"

"Naw," Calvin answered with no intention of offering an explanation for their appearance as he led Shontell through the living room to his room.

"Freaking oddballs," his roommate snapped as he picked up his game controller and turned towards the TV.

PEACHES

"I can't believe that I am serving two life sentences for crimes I didn't commit. Everyone who knows me knows that I am a strait-laced guy. I graduated college a year early from an ivy league school. I'm a deacon at my church. I have never been in trouble with the law. Hell, I've never even used alcohol or drugs. Now, I've been painted as a serial killer. Me! Conroy Jessup, one of the most generous philanthropists in Atlanta; convicted of murdering five people! I can't believe it," I explained to my cellmate, who listened unconvinced, as if I was telling him a fairytale.

Sweet's blank expression remained unimpressed. I could tell that he had heard men claim innocence thousands of times during his thirty-year sentence for killing a man who tried to rape his daughter. If there was ever a man that the criminal justice system failed, Sweet was that man. He just looked at me with tired brown eyes that matched his leathery black skin. White hair grew like cotton balls from his wide head. He was a giant of a man. I suspected around six feet three or four, and over three hundred pounds. They called him Sweet Meat. Not because of phallic praise, but because his real name was Sweetaveous Ulysses Meath III.

"Um hum," he grumbled as he chewed on an old drinking straw. "You look like you was the man."

After all the time I spent in jail awaiting the conclusion of my trial and these first few weeks in prison, I had been able to maintain my look. Every strand of my hair was in place. My hairline was straighter than an ink pen. My manicure was still intact. I looked like a million bucks in my jumpsuit. I'm still not sure if that's a good thing in prison. I don't like the way some of the men have been looking at me. Being Sweet's cellmate has kept me safe thus far. Sweet was well respected, more than that, he was feared. It also felt good to know that Sweet had no sexual interest in men whatsoever. Although his motto was *to each their own*, he frowned upon men who forced other men to bend to their interests. Pun intended.

"I know it's hard to believe, but I really am innocent. I couldn't kill a fly," I said.

"What happened then?" Sweet Meat asked in a voice that reminded me of the late great comedian Charlie Murphy. He leaned forward, feigning interest in my story, his weary eyes blinking slowly.

"I met this woman," I started as I sat down in the corner of the cell.

Sweet sat on the bottom bunk looking like he was literally dying of boredom.

"It always starts with a woman," Sweet Meat cosigned looking at me like I was a fish out of water. He curled up one side of his lip showing his cynicism.

"She was the most perfect woman I had ever seen. I know men say that all the time, but I really mean it. Peaches was incredible. Everything about her sent chills down my spine, in a good way," I exclaimed.

"Let me guess, she was a skinny white gal with blonde hair and blue eyes like yours," he mumbled.

"Actually, quite the opposite," I retorted. "Peaches was dark brown with shoulder length dreadlocks. She had the most incredible face: full lips, big beautiful eyes, high cheekbones, and a neck like a giraffe."

"Since when is a giraffe's neck good?" Sweet asked furrowing his brows.

"Her neck was long and graceful. That's all I'm saying," I replied, a little surprised that he took offense.

"Well, say that then. A giraffe's neck don't look good on nothing but a giraffe," he said. "Why you gotta compare a beautiful black woman to an animal?"

"My apologies. That was not my intention," I said, a little embarrassed by my words. The last thing I wanted Sweet to think was that I was fetishizing Peaches because I was not. I adored her and would have married her instantly if she would have accepted. After all, I did propose after the first night we slept together. I don't have an ounce of racism in me. One of my best friends, when I was a child, was black; and, according to the DNA test I got for my birthday last year, I have three percent African blood, but I knew not to say this aloud because it would have probably made Sweet even more skeptical of me.

I nervously continued, "She was beautiful. Her body was an hourglass that promised passion for infinity. Her voice was sweet and southern like Scarlet O'Hara," I chimed.

"She was a Georgia peach?" he asked.

"No, she was from Charleston," I answered as the image of her beautiful face and body filled my mind. My heartbeat quickened. I inadvertently bit my bottom lip.

"I see," Sweet Meat laughed.

"You see what?" I retorted, a bit off put by his facial expression.

"You went black and can't get back!" he rhymed like Dolomite. He slapped his giant, muscled leg and rocked back in forth.

I shook my head, slighted by him diminishing my love for Peaches to mere exotic lust. She was simply incredible. Any man with eyes could see that. I wasn't going to waste my time trying to explain myself to him. Sweet was going to believe what he wanted to believe, and it wasn't my job to change his mind.

"I met her at a charity benefit benefiting underserved inner-city children. She had raised over ten thousand dollars for the cause. I was so impressed with her that I matched her efforts plus five thousand more," I bragged.

"I hear you Mr. Big. You need to drop some coins on a brotha's books," Sweet laughed and slapped his knee again. The subject of money seemed to breathe life into his tired face.

"Keep me away from those men who keep eyeing me in the cafeteria, and I will," I promised, and I intended to keep it.

"Bet," Sweet said and extended his hand so we could shake on it. I shook his hand firmly and made a mental note to call my daughter in the morning to have her add money to Sweet's books.

"Finish telling me about Peaches," he said her name like it was illicit; making the *p* pop like a soda can.

I laughed.

"At the benefit, I asked her out on a date. At first, she was hesitant, but after I matched her fundraising efforts, she happily accepted," I stated.

"Money talks!" Sweet howled, "and BS walks!

"Yes, it does," I agreed and continued my story. "The next day, I planned a romantic night at a fancy restaurant overlooking the city. I had my car pick her up and when she arrived on the rooftop, she followed a trail of rose petals to our table."

"You doin' the most! Women don't need all that. I bet she would've been just as happy with a picnic and a date at the bookstore," Sweet said. "Women like thoughtfulness, not all that Hollywood fantasy."

I laughed under my breath. Who knew that Sweet was such a sentimental and sweet fellow? I silently disagreed. In my experience, women love Hollywood fantasy because it gives them something to brag about to their friends. Plus, it shows that a man isn't cheap. I lifted and dropped my shoulders and continued.

"I always do the most!" I exclaimed. "There was champagne, caviar, and French cuisine."

"Don't no respectable southern black woman want no fish eggs. You would have been better off serving shrimp and grits," Sweet Meat laughed.

He was right. Peaches didn't touch the caviar and barely ate her entrée.

"Our conversation flowed easily. We talked about our childhoods, our hopes and dreams. We talked about our favorite movies, our hobbies, and what makes us laugh. I felt happier than I had felt in years. An hour easily turned into four hours. After dinner, against my desire, I took her home and kissed her, on the cheek, goodnight," I said.

I leaned back against the wall reminiscing about that night. I would give my left arm to be there again. Peaches made me feel alive. Before meeting her, I was all work and no play. Burned too many times, I had given up on the concept of romantic love. My heart began to open again.

"You good homie?" Sweet asked.

I looked at him and nodded my head.

"So, what happened next?" he asked, his eyes alight with interest.

"I went home," I answered. "I went home and had the strangest dream."

"Whatchu dream?" Sweet asked.

"I was laying in my bed. Sounds of the Amazon rain forest played through my wireless speaker lulling me to sleep. Out of the corner of my eye, I saw a red wisp of smoke coming from under my door. I turned to look, but it was gone. My breathing relaxed and I focused on the sounds of the rain forest and fell asleep. Moments later, my chest felt like it was being caved in. I couldn't move. I couldn't open my eyes. I could feel my breath being sucked out of me. It felt like someone was riding my chest like a horse. My heart threatened to stop beating when the pressure left my chest and I was able to open my eyes. I sat up, heaving, teary eyed and in a panic. I had never felt anything like that in my life!" I exclaimed. The sheer memory of it all sent chills up my spine.

"Sounds like sleep paralysis," Sweet said with his eyebrow raised. "or a witch was riding you."

"That's ridiculous!" I exclaimed, shaking my head.

"Suit yourself," Sweet said nonchalantly.

"The next night, I took Peaches to a dinner with a colleague and his wife. At dinner, my colleague continuously made remarks that made Peaches uncomfortable. He sarcastically asked her questions about racially sensitive headlines in the news, made negative comments about President Obama, and an array of inappropriate comments," I said. "Honestly, I should have shut him down from the beginning, but I selfishly wanted to close a business deal, so I allowed him to continue."

"That's messed up man," Sweet said shaking his head. "Real messed up."

"I know," I admitted. "I know."

"So, what she do?" Sweet asked.

"She was gracious; a lady to the very end. She smiled and intelligently issued a rebuttal for every one of his ignorant arguments. She didn't need my help. She knew how to defend herself. By then end of the night, my colleague was schooled and dismissed. After we left the dinner, I wanted to go somewhere else. I wanted to spend more time with her, but she claimed that she was tired and wanted to go home. I knew she wasn't tired. She was just tired of being with me. I couldn't blame her. I put her in an uncomfortable situation. I apologized for my colleague's behavior and my behavior, then took her home after she agreed to let me make it up to her the next day. Later that night, I had another bout of sleep paralysis. That time it was worse than before. I was so cold, like my skin had been removed and my muscles lay bare to the elements."

Sweet raised his eyebrow.

I took a mental note of his facial expression and continued, "That night, while I slept, my colleague was murdered. The police claimed that they had video footage of me leaving my colleague's apartment minutes after the murder!" I exclaimed. "That's impossible! I was at home in my bed. I didn't go anywhere else after I took Peaches home."

"You said you felt like you were out of your skin, huh?" Sweet asked, his eyebrow still raised.

"Yeah," I answered, confused about why he was stuck on my skin after all the other things I told him. "Anyway, the next day I took Peaches to lunch at my country club. The weather was nice, so we played a round of golf and went for a walk through the garden path before we ate. Unfortunately, our waitress was a perky, young redhead named Julie who I had a short fling with a couple weeks before I met Peaches. Julie was as interesting as a cardboard box, so I broke it off after a week of lukewarm conversation and white-hot sex. I ended the affair through a short text message."

Sweet laughed. He asked, "What did you text?"

"Well, she texted me asking if I wanted to go to a movie, and I replied that I was too busy. She then asked if I wanted to come over after work, and I replied by telling her that she was a nice girl, but not for me. I wished her well and told her I would see her around. She was not thrilled, but I knew she would get over it. At least I thought she would. Apparently, that was not the case. First, she knocked a glass of water onto Peaches' lap. Then, Julie complimented Peaches' locs and asked if she could touch them. Peaches kindly said no and looked at me like I had two heads. While serving our dishes, Julie saw Peaches tuck a stray curl behind my ear. Julie said, 'Ah, how sweet! But honey, he likes it rough!', grinned sarcastically, and walked off. Peaches rolled her eyes and allowed me to explain about Julie. Peaches was understanding until I asked for the check and Julie purposely spilled hot coffee on Peaches' leg. Peaches hopped up with a scream and was two seconds from punching Julie in the face when I grabbed Peaches' arm, apologized, and escorted her out of the restaurant. Julie could be heard laughing behind us. Peaches was not happy at all. Her white shorts were ruined, and the burn on her thigh was beginning to bubble. I took her to my house and tended to her burn with my first aid kit. After her anger cooled, and the pain subsided, I had the best sex of my adult life!" I confessed and sighed. Just the thought of it made my stomach flip.

"She put it on you," Sweet laughed. "What she do?" he asked seeking the illicit details.

"A gentleman never tells," I smiled. "But I can tell you this, there was not a pleasure point on my body she did not successfully manipulate. I felt like my body was being formed from the earth for the first time and life being breathed into every pore."

"You so much drama dude," Sweet laughed.

I laughed too and said, "It was amazing! Crazy good. Leave your wife, slap your mamma good."

"Ain't nothing good enough for me to slap my mamma," Sweet said. "Carry on."

"I begged her to spend the night with me. She did. She wore me out and put me to sleep. In the middle of the night, it happened again. I was paralyzed, felt skinless, and breathless. I was afraid that Peaches would wake up and see me teary eyed and helpless, but she didn't. That same night as we slept, Julie was found dead in her apartment. She was stabbed to death and laying in a puddle of blood. The police said that Julie's roommate said that she let me enter their apartment while she was exiting. That's impossible! I spent the night with Peaches!"

"You sure about that?" Sweet questioned. "Did Peaches spend the night with you?"

"Of course, she did! She was straddling me when I woke up from my sleep paralysis. We began to make love when I opened my eyes," I barked.

"Um hum," Sweet mumbled and continued to chew on the straw which now looked like an unidentifiable piece of plastic hanging out of his mouth.

I disregarded his skepticism and continued.

"Over the course of two weeks, five of my associates were murdered. Witnesses claimed that I was in the vicinity during each of the killings. I don't know how I was pinpointed. I was home every night or at Peaches' house," I said.

"Did you have that dream every time someone you knew was murdered?" Sweet asked.

I lifted my finger to my chin and pondered. It was quite possible that I did have that awful dream every time a murder occurred.

"Do you think I was sleep walking?" I asked Sweet as if it was a viable possibility.

"I think that boo hag been walking around in your skin," Sweet said matter-of-factly.

"What the hell is a boo hag?" I screeched. I had never heard of anything so silly.

"It's that South Cackalacky witch you been running around with," Sweet replied. "Miss Peaches been wearing your skin. She rode you at night, sucked your energy, and wore your skin like a Steve Harvey suit just to get back at the people that crossed her."

I blinked my eyes slowly considering whether I was going to entertain such a ridiculous conversation. I wasn't going to, so I yawned and climbed up on my bunk.

"Thanks for listening to me Sweet," I said as I closed my eyes and forced sleep.

It wasn't long before the horrid feeling of paralysis restricted my body. A heavy weight pressed my ribs into my lungs. I couldn't breathe. I tried to cry out to Sweet, but no sound escaped my mouth. Tears formed in my eyes. I was able to crack them when the weight lifted. I turned my head towards the cell door. Something was laying on the floor. I squinted trying to make it out in the dim lighting. It looked like an inflated version of the correctional officer. My heart thumped. Fear grabbed my chest. Peaches stepped out of the shadows; the tips of her fingers hanging like ill-fitting gloves; her face off centered. I gasped.

She rubbed her arms upward and snatched her scalp to the right, adjusting her skin like long sleeves and a skull cap. She looked perfect.

"I missed you Conroy," she cooed as I sat upon the top bunk with my mouth and eyes stretched wide open.

She extended her hand for me to come to her. I sat up and backed against the wall.

"Come on," Peaches said in the most enchanting tone.

I jumped off the top bunk and landed on weak, trembling legs. Fear stopped me from taking another step.

"I won't wait forever," she smiled.

Fear froze me, but the look in her eyes melted my heart. Peaches was all I had ever wanted. I decided then and there, she could ride me until the wheels fell off. I took her hand and we were gone.

PICKLES BY THE RIVER

It takes nearly eight hours to get to New Orleans from Atlanta, and Kwame was less than twenty miles away from his destination. He was tired. With the back of his hand, he wiped the sleep from his eyes then chugged down an energy drink. It tasted like Kool-Aid made with artificial sweetener and salt. He popped his tongue and frowned while quickly blinking his eyes to fight away drowsiness as the lines on the street faded in and out of focus. He whispered a prayer for God to keep him alive and awake until he made it to his hotel room. A ragged sigh escaped his lips as his foot pressed down on the pedal.

It had been a long and arduous day. After a self-imposed ten-hour shift, he went home, gathered his luggage, and jumped into his car. Kwame was exhausted, but there was no way he was going to miss the Bayou Classic. The legendary college football game between Southern University and Grambling State was the annual highpoint of the year for him and his alumni friends. It was a time to unwind, catch up, and have some fun. Plus, he had too much money riding on the game and he truly looked forward to homecoming. There was nothing in the world as amazing as a HBCU homecoming. It had been over a decade since he had seen his college buddies. Life, family, and work had kept him away. Now, there was nothing in the world that could get in his way. He was determined to laugh, turn up, dance, and live his best life. Kwame couldn't remember the last time that he had fun. Fun was as foreign to him as China.

A wild party, a stiff drink, and a one-night stand is what he needed after the year that he had experienced. His wife had passed away nine months earlier in a car accident. Grief crippled him almost every second of the day. A lifetime of love and happiness crumbled in a millisecond. Uncertainty and loneliness filled him like an overstuffed clothes hamper. It took every ounce of his will to even consider going to New Orleans.

The six-figure job he had since his late twenties, was abruptly snatched away by a company merger. Years of hard work had been reduced to a plaque and severance pay. The only positive thing about being laid off was that it forced him to follow his dream of becoming a business owner. Now he worked himself to the bone for his own dream instead of someone else's, and it felt good.

His apartment caught fire two months ago causing him to move back in with is mother. There was nothing more tragic than a grown man living with his mother. His only child had just graduated from college and moved across the pond leaving him in the loneliest state he had ever known. To make matters worse, he was intoxicated with cough syrup to ease the agony of the flu, and he had lost his great grandfather's watch. That watch had been in his family for over two hundred years, and he lost it after the fire. All in all, his life sucked at the moment, but he didn't care. He was going to have fun no matter what.

Kwame pressed his foot hard on the gas and zoomed across I-10 towards the Davis "Naturally N'Awlins" Memorial Bridge. The absurdly long bridge made most drivers nervous, but not Kwame. The bridge gave him butterflies because he knew how close he was to his destination. In less than half an hour, he pulled into his hotel's parking lot and unloaded his car. He checked in and headed straight to the shower.

The hot shower washed away his cares as he stood reflecting on his drive. He exited and toweled off before he climbed under the cold sheets to welcome sleep.

Loud ringing startled him from his sleep.

"Hello," he groggily answered the phone.

The clock on the nightstand showed nine o'clock pm.

"Mr. Murry, this is your wake-up call," the voice on the other end of the receiver replied.

"Thanks," he said and hung up the phone.

He threw the covers off himself and stood up; his well-made nude form --a splash of ebony against the backdrop of the room. Within minutes, he was dressed, and his thick, kinky hair groomed. He brushed his teeth and smiled proudly in the mirror admiring their white perfection. Kwame pulled his cell phone from his pocket. The large rectangle lit up illuminating his face. He unlocked it and found the contact he needed.

"Aye Terrence! What up man?" Kwame asked.

"Wain' on you brah," Terrence answered with a laugh behind his words. Music and laughter vibrated in the background.

"Sounds like ya'll got started without me," Kwame retorted.

"You know how it goes," Terrence laughed. "We heading to the club. You in?"

"Hell yeah! I'm in! You think I drove all the way from Atlanta to sit in this hotel room?" Kwame replied. "Text me the address."

"Bet," said Terrence before hanging up the phone.

Within seconds, the text with the club's address came through Kwame's phone. He downed half a bottle of cold medicine, grabbed his jacket and exited the room in a flash.

The streets of the French Quarter were bustling. College students and middle-aged partiers alike, wandered in and out of local bars on wobbly knees. Tap dancing children with money filled hats and makeshift marching bands crowded every corner adding to the ear-thumping clamor. Red lights shined atop the doors of clubs of ill repute as their exotic dancers flittered in and out wearing naughty lingerie. Voodoo shops, real and commercial, were tucked in between the bars beckoning the spiritually curious to enter.

Kwame pushed his way through the crowd as he followed the GPS on his phone. Although he had a great sense of direction and knew Canal Street like the back of his hand, there were so many clubs and bars in The Quarter and the crowd was so thick, he would be looking for his friends all night if he were to rely on his own instincts.

Periodically, an eerie chill ran down his arms. Kwame always felt that New Orleans was a breathing city. It was a living entity that one could feel like one could feel the wind or the rain. It was hard to explain the pulse that beat through the streets of New Orleans. The easiest way to put it was to say that the city was preternatural. People called it a haunted town, but Kwame felt New Orleans itself was a spirit. The atmosphere clung to his skin, seeped through his pores, and tickled his nerve endings ever so lightly. The feeling was both eerie and exciting. It was unequivocally New Orleans.

The GPS told Kwame that he had arrived at his destination. He looked up at the neon sign above his head. It read, *Mami Wata's Watering Hole.* He pushed through the crowd and managed to make it through the front door. The place was packed from wall to wall. Loud music and slurring voices scented with potent daiquiris bounced off the walls. Ladies rolled their hips, to the music, against men sweating and pumping behind them. Beads, feathers, and confetti littered the floor. Kwame zigzagged his way to the bar and luckily found an empty stool next to a striking ebony woman admiring herself in a hand mirror. He sat down next to her and pulled his cell phone from his pocket to shoot Terrence a text to let him know that he had arrived and was waiting at the bar. Kwame stuck his phone back into his jean pocket and turned to the woman next to him.

"Hello beautiful. Whatcha drinkin'?" he asked while flashing a perfect smile.

The woman parted her bright red lips and smiled back. Her honey colored eyes, which made him feel like gravity was failing, against her charcoal skin sent a strange chill up his arms then down the sides of his back. He shook it off, trying hard to hide his unease. She was very attractive but had a peculiar air about her. Thick black coils crowned her head like ebony sunbeams shooting towards the sky. A two-headed emerald snake with ruby eyes decorated her neck. Kwame found the necklace unnerving. He could have sworn the gemstone serpent moved with a life of its own. He swallowed hard and dismissed the foolish thought. The cold medicine must have been kicking in.

"Mango tequila," she replied with an accent he had never heard before. It sounded African, Caribbean, and Louisiana creole all in one. There was a seductive twang to it that sang to his very soul.

Kwame cleared his throat and raised his hand to get the bartender's attention.

A young woman, with dirty blonde hair and violet eyes, leaned over the counter to take his order. Kwame ordered two mango tequilas and turned his attention back to the woman next to him.

"What's your name?" he asked, unsuccessfully avoiding direct eye contact. He felt if he looked into her eyes too long, he would literally float away and be gone forever. "My name is Kwame. My friends call me Kwam."

"My name is whatever you want it to be," she replied flashing an enchanting smile. Fire danced in her eyes.

"I want it to be whatever it is plus my last name," he quipped while clinking glasses with her in a silent toast to the promise of a very sexy night. They both took a sip.

"You're a smooth talker," she cooed.

Kwame was amazed that he could hear her voice so clearly over the crowd and loud music. It was almost as if she was speaking telepathically. Her words echoed through his head.

"Seriously, what's your name?" he asked before taking another sip. The drink was very strong but good. He drank some more.

She smiled but said nothing.

Kwame wasn't going to ask again. If it didn't matter to her, it didn't matter to him. Maybe it was better he didn't know her name anyway; no strings attached.

"What brings you to New Orleans?" she asked while raising her hand to catch the bartender's attention.

Kwame answered, "How do you know I'm visiting? Maybe I'm from here."

The woman laughed aloud.

"Impossible!" she yelped.

The blonde woman skipped over almost immediately and said, "Yes, Mami Wata?"

"Fix me a drink to go, and a kosher dill," Mami Wata replied.

The bartender mixed a drink and poured it into a to-go cup, then pulled a giant pickle jar from under the counter. She took an ice pick, pulled out two fat pickles, and placed them in a sandwich bag.

"One for your guest," the bartender said as she handed Mami Wata the pickles and drink.

"I don't like pickles," Kwame said as he took another sip.

"You'll like this one," Mami Wata replied.

Kwame silently protested. He refused to let a debate about pickles get in the way of a possible steamy night with one of the most enthralling women he had ever seen.

"So, this is your spot?" Kwame asked.

"Yes, it is." she answered.

Kwame nodded and looked around at the high-end furniture, large flat screen TVs, the shiny chrome beer taps, and the art on the walls, then looked at her immaculately groomed hair, nails, and clothes. He should have known. She looked like she not only owned the place, but the world.

"What kind of name is Mami Wata? Where are you from?"

"Let's get out of here and go somewhere quiet," she requested.

"I'm waiting to meet my friends," he said as she stood up from her barstool and stood between his legs. She locked eyes with him. Feeling himself floating again, he looked to the right to break the trance. He allowed his eyes to rest on the smooth blue-black skin of her face, admired her large slanted eyes, then allowed his eyes to admire her body.

Kwame's heart pounded against his t-shirt. He could feel the heat from her skin drifting towards him. She smelled of waterfalls and flowers. Her body was extraordinary; lean, strong, but curvy in all the right places. She was taller than he imagined; standing at least six feet tall, when Kwame stood up, they were almost eye to eye.

"Are you ready to go?" she asked locking her free hand with his.

"Let me text my friends," he replied as he tapped out a text with his thumb and put the phone back in his pocket. He laced fingers with hers and followed her out of the bar.

Canal Street was a traffic jam of people. Kwame and Mami Wata pushed their way through the crowd until they turned off Bourbon

Street. The crowd was just as thick and loud as before. They picked up the pace until they turned on Toulouse Street; then, slowed into a relaxing stroll.

"You never told me where you're from," Kwame said as they faded in and out of the crowd. He felt like he was screaming but her expression indicated that she could hear him okay. The smell of liquor and vomit drifted on a breeze. Light from the full moon illuminated her skin. She almost looked ethereal; like the light shined through her not just reflected off her. For a second, Kwame thought her snake necklace moved again laying one of its heads comfortably between her breasts.

"I'm from the sea," she replied with a strange smirk. "The water has always been my home. I've lived off the coast of Africa, the Caribbean, and right here in the gulf."

"No wonder your accent is so different. I can hear all those areas in your voice. It's beautiful," he said.

"Thank you," she smiled.

"My father used to have a houseboat. He loved the water so much that if my mother would have allowed it, we would have been from the sea too," he said. "We used to go sailing every year."

"Sounds like fun," she replied. "I'm surprised we've never met before."

Kwame raised his brow. She looked like she was serious. They didn't live in the same city, never attended the same schools, or ran with the same crowd. Where would they have met, in the ocean? He found the idea ridiculous. He chuckled.

"Once when I was a kid, I thought I saw a face staring back at me from the water. My mother, who was Jamaican, told me there was a fish that the fisherman swore had a human face. They would cut the head off and throw it back into the sea before coming to shore. The body of the fish they would sell. I found that story disturbing on so many levels because I wouldn't ever want to eat a fish with a person's face. It's like eating *The Little Mermaid*. Kinda cannibalistic too," he laughed lackadaisically. "Enough about me, tell me about you."

"No, I'm enjoying the sound of your voice. Your eyes tell me that you need to talk. Have you been having a hard time lately?" Mami Wata asked.

They arrived at Toulouse Station at the river front.

"Follow me," she said as she walked towards the Mississippi River.

"We should have gone through Woldennberg Park. It's nicer there," he commented as he reluctantly followed.

"There are too many people over there. I have a special spot," she said as she led him to a small tuft of high vegetation.

Kwame slowed down. The thought of going into high grass by the river was not appetizing. There was no telling what kind of humongous bugs, funky trash, or dead bodies could be tucked in there.

Kwame stopped and said, "I think I've gone as far as I'm going to go."

She turned to look at him, her eyes like dancing flames in the moonlight. "Trust me," she whispered without moving her mouth. He heard her clearly and his feet began to move again. She parted the brush and before them was a bed of red and white flowers. The furthest edge of the flowers dipped into the water like the toes of nymphs.

"Come," she invited him to sit beside her. She removed her shoes and her feet disappeared beneath the petals.

Kwame sat down beside her. The moonlight, the flowers' fragrance, and the woman made him forget about the toxicity of the river, the possibility of insects, or the dangers that may be lurking in the shadows.

She handed him a pickle.

"I don't like…"

"Just taste it," she said as she handed him the wet cucumber.

Kwame bit into the pickle. The sour flavor permeated his mouth. He frowned.

She shrugged her shoulders and laughed. "I tried," she said.

He spat the pickle out and leaned back into the flowers. She removed his shoes to let the Mississippi kiss his toes.

"I must really like you because I would have never come this close to the river on my own," Kwame said. "And you must be fine because I hate pickles!"

"You look like you needed some rest and relaxation. Your spirit seems troubled," she said between chewing; pickle juice glossing her lips.

"You a voodoo woman?" Kwame asked with one brow raised. "I'm not into that stuff, so if you have cat bones in your purse or want to read my palm, don't waste your time."

Mami Wata laughed aloud.

"No," she replied. "Not at all."

He rested his head on her lap and looked up into her eyes. They glowed in the moonlight like the eyes of werewolves he saw in old horror movies when he was a kid. A shiver ran down his spine. Despite his uneasiness, the warmth of her lap was too inviting to move away.

"Tell Mami what's on your mind," she purred as she finished her pickle then started on the rejected one.

Kwame started to protest. He was not about to lay down his troubles on her and risk not getting laid. He had not been touched by a woman in so long that he might explode if she held his hand too long. The mere warmth of her lap made his insides squirm. He thanked God he chose to wear jeans instead of jogging pants.

"Nothing is on my mind," he lied as he tried to banish away thoughts of his late wife, lost job, distant child, and fire ravished home.

"Come now," she whispered. "You can talk to me." Mami Wata twirled his hair with her fingers then ran her finger down the side of his face. Butterflies did summersaults in his stomach. He opened his mouth to decline her offer, but all his woes came spilling out. Kwame told her everything until tears began to wet his eyes. Surprisingly, he was not embarrassed but felt comforted and spiritually lifted. It was like his skin had shed and fell off leaving him feeling like a new man. After his confessions, she kissed him on the forehead and stood up; her spikey hair, eclipsing the moon, casting a shadow across his face. Yet, her eyes still shined like fireflies suspended in midair.

"Let's go for a swim." She pulled him up from the ground as if he weighed nothing. She quickly disrobed until she was wearing nothing but moonlight and her necklace. The sight of her body jumpstarted his heart and paralyzed his mind. He quickly stripped; ignoring the fact that he was agreeing to go nude into the murky Mississippi. He followed her into the cool, muddy waters like a trusting child. Waves licked her legs until they disappeared beneath the waters. She pulled him in until they both stood waist deep.

She wrapped her arms around his neck and looked into his eyes. His hands found her hips; fearing if they had not, he would float away into the firmament. She kissed him softly. Mami Wata pressed her chest to his and with a little hop, wrapped her legs around his waist. Kwame sighed loudly. The warmth of her body made his head swoon.

Eyes locked, skin pressed together, her fingers ran up and down his back. Her hips rolled against him like waves of water. She unlocked her legs and let them float beneath the whitecaps. Kwame's eyes showed panic. His dream of making love to her was quickly fading. He reached into the water for one of her legs hoping to wrap them back around him. Instead of a leg, his hand grabbed something slippery and thick. He looked down. A giant fishtail glistened beneath the waves. In confusion, he stepped backwards. The tail blended seamlessly into Mami Wata's torso. The necklace on her neck elongated into a life-sized serpent which coiled around her arms from fingertip to fingertip; their heads resting in the palms of her hands. Her eyes ignited then cooled. A smile curled her crimson lips.

Kwame could not move. The waves of the Mississippi crashed against his back, yet he stood as still as a stone pillar.

"I wish you no harm my love," she cooed. "Only hope and a future of prosperity."

Kwame stared at her unblinking. He believed that he must have drank too much; that his imagination was getting the best of him; that he had fallen asleep in her lap and they were still relaxing on the shore.

"I called you to me to ease your broken heart," she sang to the rhythm of the river's waves. "Promise to love me forever, and your future will far exceed your past."

Kwame forgot to breathe.

"I require your fidelity once per year. Come back to me every season and your life will be grand. Break your promise and you'll beg for death," Mami Wata sang, her serpent hissing in the background harmonizing with her voice.

Kwame nodded. He didn't know why he nodded, but he did.

Mami Wata reached down into the waters and came up with an old pocket watch dangling from a gold chain.

"That's my watch!" Kwame exclaimed, surprising himself by the outburst. He reached out his hand and she dropped the watch into it.

"Everything lost will be found again," Mami Wata promised. "If you are true to me."

Eyes locked on the watch, Kwame nodded his head again.

"Come to me," she cooed. The serpent recoiled and shrank back into an emerald necklace. Her iridescent tail divided and transformed into two ebony legs.

Kwame watched silently; chest heaving and mind spinning.

Mami Wata took him by the hand and led him back to shore where they made love on the flower bed; the sweet-scented petals embracing their skin as they embraced each other. Sleep followed ecstasy.

When Kwame opened his eyes, she was gone, the flowers were gone, and he was fully dressed. He checked his phone. Terrence had left a text instructing Kwame to meet them on the corner of Canal and Bourbon in ten minutes. None of the previous text messages were in his phone. No address to *Mami Wata's Watering Hole*. Nothing! Kwame looked at the time. Strangely, it was only twenty minutes since he last talked to Terrence.

"Impossible!" Kwame sighed. "I must be drunk as hell! What was in that drink?"

There was no sign of Mami Wata anywhere. There was only one set of footprints in the mud. He did an internet search for her bar and there was no place listed.

Kwame got up from the ground, dusted himself off, and made his way to Bourbon Street. A group of men stood on the corner laughing, drinking, and flirting with women who were laughing, drinking and flirting as much as they were. Upon sight, he ran to his boys and greeted them all with a hug. They reciprocated, then turned into the nearest bar.

"Drinks for the homies!" he yelled.

His friends cheered.

"Plain orange juice for me," he whispered to a tall and wispy looking male bartender. There was no way Kwame needed more liquor after the brain hiccup he had just had. Adding insanity to his list of woes was not an option.

Terrence came over to Kwame and whispered into his ear, "You sure you wanna treat? I know you've been having a hard time lately. Let me get it."

"I'm good man," Kwame replied. It was true, he didn't have the money to treat but he was going to put it on his credit card. He'd worry about the debt later. It was homecoming weekend. He deserved a splurge.

"Okay brother," Terrence said and turned towards the other fellows with his glass lifted.

"Hey," Kwame called out and grabbed Terrence's arm.

Terrence leaned in so he could hear better.

"Did you ever send me that address to the club?" Kwame asked, unable to accept that he may have imagined his experience with Mami Wata.

"Naw, we couldn't decide on where to go. That's why I told you to meet us on the corner," Terrence mumbled as he guzzled a bottle of beer.

Kwame shook his head. The whole experience with Mami Wata must have been a fabrication brought on by sleep deprivation and stress. Worry began to sneak up on him, but he forced it away. Nothing was going to get in the way of him having a good time.

"Another round!" Kwame yelled as he picked up his juice and began to do the two-step to a hip-hop song blasting through the bar.

Kwame reached into his pocket for his wallet to ensure that his business credit card was in it so he could guarantee that he wouldn't have to take Terrence up on his offer to pay. The embarrassment alone may send Kwame to his grave. He opened his wallet. A large wad of cash was inside. He couldn't hide the shock on his face if he tried. He dug deeper into his pocket and pulled out his great grandfather's pocket watch.

"What the…" he started when two flashes of light caught his eye. Across the room. Mami Wata sat at a table, her golden eyes sparkling. She shot him a smile while lifting her glass.

"Until next year my love, "she whispered without words and vanished.

REMINISCING

I arrived in Atlanta in 1932. It was at high noon. The sun didn't bother me much because an old gris gris woman back home taught me how to make a salve to protect my skin. She even taught me how to make eyedrops to protect my eyes from the sun. It was cold. I remember that it was cold because I wore a fox shawl; the kind of shawl where the foxes were connected by mouth and tail as if they died trying to eat each other. It was given to me by a nice white lady, named Mrs. Hatterick, that I used to work for back in Sparta, GA. I taught her daughter piano lessons, which was a rare job for a colored woman during that time; however, I was a musical prodigy. I knew how to play any instrument I touched. Music came as naturally to me as walking and talking. That natural ability helped ensure that I, a woman with no family, didn't have to struggle. Mrs. Hatterick payed me well and referred new business to me often. My success was her success. It gave her joy to see me do well.

In Atlanta, it didn't take me long to make friends after I found a room in a large boarding house off Wheat Street in the inner city. My room was in a house of single women. One had to be careful when finding boarding homes; whore houses masqueraded as group homes as often as birds flew across the sky. Big Mama Clementine, an elderly woman who we all affectionally called Ma Tine, owned the home. She was a self-made woman who accumulated an impressive amount of wealth by selling hot plates of food to neighborhood laborers. During lunch time, the food line would stretch from Ma Tine's door down five or six blocks. Dirt caked, sweat drenched men stood laughing and talking as they waited patiently for their turn. Ma Tine, who was the color of butterscotch candy, as thin as a branch of sugar cane, and as tall as a pine tree, ran her operation so fast and smooth that the men in front of the line could get back in the line for seconds and be back to work on time.

She was married to a kind man we called Grandpa Pete, who had died way before any of us arrived on Ma Tine's doorstep. We knew him by the numerous photos around the house. Ma Tine talked about him like he was still living in the house. Anytime something went missing, she would yell, "Pete, you betta stop playin'!"

I met Ma Tine my first day in Atlanta. She was friends with a friendly woman I met at a dress shop where I was looking for work. While I was outlining my skills to the surly woman behind the counter, Ma Tine came waltzing in the door like a giant dancer. Her long legs stretched across the entire store in three steps. Dressed to the nines with matching hat, gloves, and heels, Ma Tine was the most eloquent woman I had ever laid eyes on, but when she opened her mouth, the most ill-bred chopped up English bent her tongue. I thought she was speaking another language. It took me a few minutes to catch the rhythm of her words; when I did, understanding her was fairly easy.

"Missa Mercy, whatchoo got fo' me taday?" Ma Tine asked the store owner.

Miss Mercy, a short pudgy woman who was the color of a cinnamon oatmeal cookie, walked from behind the counter with a grin so big that it looked painted on. She grabbed Ma Tine by the hand and led her to a couch before presenting the store's new arrivals.

Ma Tine looked over the dresses, examined the fabric --every stitch, ran her fingers over the silks and laces.

I watched, intrigued by her meticulousness. My stare caught her attention. She paused and looked me up and down like I was on the auction block.

"Who dat?" she asked Miss Mercy who was kneeling at Ma Tine's feet delicately slipping a bright red heel onto it.

"She lookin' for work Ms. Clementine. She new here. Her people from Sparta," Miss Mercy replied with a thick southern drawl.

"Whatcho name gal?" Ma Tine asked, her thin wavy hair hanging from the bottom of her hat like fringes on a lampshade.

"June Mae ma'am. June Mae Proctor," I replied and extended my hand. She shook it like she was afraid to touch it, like I just emptied a slop jar or someone's spit cup.

"You showl is purdy to be black as tar. Ya eva thank 'bout straightenin' yo hair? All dat thick hair would lay down real nice," Ma Tine backhand complimented my black skin and kinky hair. I wasn't offended. She didn't know any better. Centuries of dehumanization could do that to a people; make a people forget who they truly are; make them forget their divinity. She was whitewashed; her esteem tied to her bright skin and see-through hair. In the eyes of those who hated colored people so vehemently, she was just as black as I was. Little did she understand, that hate stemmed from covetousness.

"Thank you," I replied with a polite curtsy.

"You got purdy eyes too. What color dat is?" Ma Tine asked, leaning closer with squinted eyes.

"They change according to my mood," I answered. It was true. My eyes changed from light brown to a yellowish green. The flecks of colors within them usually unnerved people. Back home they called me rainbow eyes.

"I ain't neva seen no eyes like dat!" Ma Tine exclaimed. "If you wasn't so nice I'd thank ya had da devil in ya. Dem eyes somethin' else. Ain't day Missa Mercy?"

"Yes ma'am," Miss Mercy nodded while bringing out an array of hats.

"Where ya' stayin' at gal?" Ma Tine asked as she shook the red shoe off her foot and stuck her foot out for Miss Mercy to put on a green shoe with a large satin bow on the top.

"Nowhere ma'am," I confessed. "I just got off the train about an hour ago. I'm looking for work and a place to stay."

"Well Missa Mercy, give dis gal a job!" Ma Tine demanded.

"Yes ma'am," Miss Mercy said as she rang up two dresses and a pair of shoes. It was obvious that Ma Tine was one of her best customers.

"It ain't safe fo' no woman ta be out in da streets. A purdy young thang like you is good for gettin'. Shiftless niggas'll have ya turnin' tricks like a clown at da circus and I ain't havin' it! You comin' home wit' me," Ma Tine declared. "Dats it. No mo' ta say."

"Yes ma'am," I replied with a crooked smile. I liked her instantly. She was a good person. Kindness, pride, and honesty pulsated from her skin. She was an immediate friend; a mother. A mother that I never had.

I had no fear of being on the streets. There were few people who had the ability to do me harm, but I graciously accepted her invitation. Being in a cozy house beat out sleeping on a park bench any day.

I had to speed walk to keep pace with Ma Tine's long legs. I followed her about six blocks to a lovely two-story home. An eloquently manicured lawn was the precursor to the beautifully furnished home. Once we entered, Ma Tine called through the house and a handful of women came running into the living room like the house was on fire.

"Dis is our new house guest. She ain't got no people so we huh people," Ma Tine said.

The women came and introduced themselves one by one with a welcoming hug and a warm smile. There was about six of them. The youngest about thirteen and the oldest around forty. I took a liking to Gretchen, a mild-mannered mulatto from Louisiana in her mid-twenties. She became my life partner, the sister I never had.

The years passed fast living in Ma Tine's house. Life was as good as it could get. We felt safe and secure with a healthy measure of happiness. We shared resources and secrets. We were family in every sense. The number of girls shrank from seven to four due to two marriages and Ella Mae, the youngest, going off to college. Everything was perfect, until Alice came.

Alice Haywood was a troubled woman. A professional drug addict and drunk, she cursed like a sailor and fought like a man. Tiny Terror is what they called her. At four feet eleven inches and eighty-nine pounds, medium brown complexion with thick curly hair, her pocketknife sliced faster than a deli blade. She was ugly. She had a long nose, thin lips and eyes too far apart. Dressed and looked like a teenaged boy save for giant breasts that made her look like she would topple over at any time, she was agitable, mean, and hellbent on revenge. Word on the street was that she killed both of her parents when she was a teen because they were a pair of junkies who prostituted her out. She was mad at the world and the world was mad at her. Of course, none of this mattered to Ma Tine. She could not stand to see a woman on the streets, so she took Alice into our home and allowed all hell to break loose. Alice brought nothing but chaos and disorder. From her junkie girlfriends and boyfriends to brutal fights to illegal gambling to Alice pimping her girlfriends out to her boyfriends when she got broke. We found peace when she was in jail and our countenances fell when she came back home. Alice was a pile of pain and foolery stacked high and ready to tumble over. She made her money by running numbers and lost it by gambling. Alice was adamant about traveling down the road to perdition.

Alice and I avoided each other for the most part. I didn't like her, and she didn't like me. When she went to the left, I went to the right. It didn't take a second after meeting to realize that she and I did not mix. She resented my secretive calm. She often called me a devil witch. She claimed that I was a demon. She spread lies about my whereabouts late at night. She pointed out that I never ate or drank, that no one really knew my age. Alice felt that I knew way too much for a young woman, that I was wise beyond my years. She claimed that no one was that educated. She pointed out that my eyes twinkled like they were made of glitter, and my skin was always cold. She claimed that I had the power of mind control. If this were true, I would have made her leave the moment she arrived. Her ravings began to put doubt in the hearts of some of the girls. I could tell by the way some of them pulled away from me, the way they began to watch me closely. I didn't care. Gretchen and Ma Tine still loved me. That's all that mattered. I ignored Alice, but I abhorred her disrespectful constant acting out. Numerous times I begged Ma Tine to kick Alice out of the house, but Ma would not listen. She clung to the false idea that love could change anyone. I was old enough to know that some people were rotten from the inside out. Love, in all its power, could not resurrect the truly dead. I was willing to leave Alice be until she set her eyes on Gretchen.

Gretchen was quiet and very shy. An orphan from birth, she became accustomed to getting the short end of the stick causing her to become withdrawn and unable to stand up for herself. When we first met, she was so timid that she barely talked, now she was more confident and willing to speak up when needed, but still very shy. This made Alice the perfect bully. She would throw mud on Gretchen's fresh laundry, bump into her in the hallway causing her to fall. She stole money from Gretchen; spit in her face and dared her to retaliate. Alice even slept with the man Gretchen was in love with. Alice claimed that it was unnatural for Gretchen to be a thirty-year-old virgin. Alice felt justified in sleeping with the man because she felt she was trying to help the poor guy. Alice even offered to sleep with Gretchen, but she rebuked Alice and prayed for her immortal soul.

I tried to take up for Gretchen as much as I could, but I was not always home. It was unfeasible for me to be.

One-night Alice came home high; completely out of her mind. The rubber band from her last heroine injection was still tied around her arm. When she stumbled in, a tall, scruffy, Irish cop stumbled in behind her; his greasy red hair slick to his head under his hat; freckles speckled across his ruddy, pale face.

In the middle of the living room, he backhand slapped Alice to the floor. He yelled something about his number dropping and not getting his money. He pulled her up from the floor and slapped her down again. Expletives bounced off the walls as he called her every foul name he could think of. Ma Tine came out of the back of the house with a pistol in her hand. She told the cop to leave if he wanted to keep his head. He said he wasn't going anywhere without his money.

I watched quietly from the hallway. No one knew I was home. I had heard the commotion from outside and came in through the second-story window. I remained quiet. I wanted no questions.

The girls came from the other end of the house hollering and crying, begging the police officer to let Alice go. The cop kicked Alice in the ribs and raised his big booted foot to stump down on her head when Gretchen screamed out for mercy. The filthy cop looked up at Gretchen with a snaggle toothed grin.

Alice saw the cop's smitten glare and screamed out, "She's one of my girls. Let me go and you can have her!"

"No!" Gretchen screamed. "I am a Christian woman!"

The police officer grabbed Gretchen's arm and drug her out of the house kicking and screaming while Ma Tine cursed and threatened to blow his head off. She and the officer knew she didn't have the heart to pull the trigger. Alice cried, slumped over on the floor bleeding profusely. The girls covered their ears as Gretchen's screams cut through the air.

I left the house.

The officer threw Gretchen into the backseat of his police car and slammed the door.

Laying on the seat and sobbing uncontrollably, a movement caught her eye. She looked down. Her sobs were stifled. My eyes flashed. I placed my finger to my lips demanding silence. She obeyed.

The car pulled into a dark alley. Brick walls stank of urine and liquor. The sound of rats scurrying through trash made my skin crawl. He opened the back door.

"Ready for me little lady," he laughed and reached for his belt buckle.

Like a serpent, my body twisted from the floor. I stood before him in a matter of seconds. A hiss escaped my mouth as I bared my fangs before sinking them into his pink, meaty neck. Blood rushed into my mouth like hot copper; its taste --an orgasm on my tongue. I drank until his neck caved in like an inflated dumpling, then dropped his sloppy wet body to the ground like the garbage he was.

I turned to Gretchen, mouth dripping in crimson life. Instead of fear, I saw wonder. Instead of damnation, I saw admiration. She smiled at me, hands folded and eyes bright and shining.

"Make me strong like you," she cried. "I never want to be weak again."

Normally, I would have refused. I would have bid her goodbye and disappeared from her life, but her eyes were broken and desperate. Her tears leaked the kind of desperation that led to eventual suicide. The blood gift would be her liberation. Who was I not to set her free? She was my friend and I was lonely, so I drank from her wrist and allowed her to drink from mine. I watched as her brown eyes became speckled with color. I watched every bruise and scratch, on her body, heal. I watched her become like me.

Hand and hand, we walked home in silence. I knew that she was reveling in her newfound sensory perception, sharpened sight and hearing. The tickle of the wind on her immortal skin. I couldn't wait until she discovered her speed and ability to climb.

When we arrived at the house, Alice was stumbling out of the door with a suitcase in hand. Ma Tine had finally put her out.

Gretchen squeezed my hand. I knew she was angry, even more, she was hungry. Her insides roared. Her fangs cut her bottom lip. Her tongue lapped up the blood as she released a voracious sigh.

Alice looked up at us we watched her stumble down the walkway with a wine bottle in her hand. Her tiny face was swollen on one side. Her thin legs bent at the knees.

"Finally got that cherry popped huh?" she grumbled with an aching laugh and took a sip out of the bottle.

Gretchen let go of my hand. In a blink of an eye, she was sucking blood out of Alice like a straw; her tiny body bobbing under the pressure of Gretchen's fangs. I watched. I couldn't summon emotions. I had none. Gretchen dropped Alice to the ground and went inside the house. The house was dark so it was a good chance that she would go unnoticed.

I disposed of the body and went back home where we stayed for many happy years until our ageless bodies looked like an oddity.

I closed my journal and placed it back into the dust covered box in which I found it, then placed the box back on the top attic shelf. I mourned the past. Years flew by on hummingbird wings. All the ladies I had loved had returned to the dust; became vague characters in a past life production. I had long left the red hills of Georgia for the icy winds of Chicago then went to the palm trees of southern California. Now, I'll bask on the beaches of Miami until my undying youth is made apparent. New friends and family occupy my time. Hopes of love died with my lovers. It is not my path. The pain is too great. I find joy in my sisterhood with Gretchen. Eternity is ours.

My cell phone rang, wrenching me from reminiscing. It was Gretchen. I was making us late for our friend's wedding. I hit ignore. I had no desire for an ear lashing. I grabbed my car keys, told the smart speaker to turn off the lights, and drove to meet my best friend. In a half a day, we will be back where it all started; the transformative streets of Atlanta.

SAMSON AND DELILAH

"I'm outta marshmallow root," Delilah grumbled as she picked up an empty glass jar and shook it. She placed it back into her apothecary cabinet and slowly turned to her husband who was sitting at a table topped with an assortment of herbs, roots, jars of liquid, and creamy balms.

"Can you go get me some more? Lula Bell will be here tomorrow to pick up her ointment. I promised to fix her something to take the swelling out her feet. Run down to the health food store in Little Five Points and pick up some marshmallow and some devil's claw root too," Delilah asked, her full lips covered in bright red lipstick, her hair wrapped in vividly colored fabric. Although she was still quite pretty, the wrinkles in her onyx face made her look at least two hundred years old. The neighborhood people often joked that she was. She and her husband seemed to be a permanent fixture in the community that outdated most people's great grandparents.

"Okay," Samson replied, his wrinkled mouth turned downward. "Make sure that's all ya need 'cause I ain't goin' back out once I get back in," he continued in a thick southern drawl. He grumbled something about his aching knees and always having to make runs to the store under his breath.

Delilah rolled her eyes.

Samson looked even older than Delilah with white hair shooting from the top of his head like dandelion seeds and green eyes deep and yellowed by time. His high yellow skin revealed blue and green veins and his curved back reminded most people of Quasimodo. His pale skin gave him the illusion of mixed heritage, but the only ancestry he claimed was from the powerful southern black men who raised him. He slowly pushed himself up from the chair, his thin frame looking deceptively frail. He walked over to his wife and reached out his big wrinkled hand for her car keys.

Delilah grunted as she maneuvered her short round frame off the stool she sat on. Homemade knee-high stockings held up by hand tied knots covered the bottom of her legs which were as big as tree trunks. Her dress looked like a multicolored tent and the apron she wore was stained with all kinds of concoctions. She walked over to a nearby shelf and snatched up a purse whose leather was as wrinkled and lined as she was. She reached in, dug around for a while, and came out with car keys. She handed them to him. He closed his hand around hers and kissed the back of her hand. Delilah blushed.

"Get outta here, you old fool, before you start something you can't finish," she jested.

Samson laughed as he spun on his heels, in slow motion, as fast as someone over a century year old could spin and hurried out of the house. He climbed into an old Chevy and pulled out the driveway, spinning his wheels, headed to Sevananda on Moreland Avenue.

Delilah opened her apothecary cabinet to take inventory of her herbs when a loud knock on the door startled her so badly that she dropped a jar on the floor, splattering a tincture all over her feet. Delilah hissed a few cuss words, stepped over the mess, and made her way to the front door. She looked through the peephole and saw a young woman standing on the porch shuffling her feet and looking over her shoulder. The woman was tall and well-built with a delicate face that was strangely familiar and thick kinky hair that crowned her head like a lion's mane. She wore a t-shirt that read, *ATL Ho!* Desperation pulsated from her eyes. Delilah reluctantly opened the door.

"Yeah," Delilah said as she stuck her head through the crack.

"You gotta help me!" the woman whined.

"I ain't gotta do nothing. Who are you and what are you doing at my door?" Delilah asked with furrowed brows. She didn't like opening the door for strangers. There were too many people in her neighborhood willing to do something strange for some change.

"Please Mrs. Delilah. My granny said that you're the only one who can help me," the woman pled. "Please!"

"Who is your granny?" Delilah asked opening the door wide and standing with folded arms. The woman looked too young for Delilah to know her grandmother. Only a select few knew the special workings of Samson and Delilah and this woman wasn't one of them.

"Johnnie Ruth Foster," the woman replied, tears forming in her eyes as she searched her surroundings.

Delilah's mouth dropped open. She grabbed her chest and stepped backwards.

"How can that be?" Delilah muttered. "Roofie has been dead for sixty years! How do you know her?"

Johnnie Ruth was one of Delilah's best friends back in the day. They used to eat chicken at Pascal's every Sunday when Vine City was the mecca of the Civil Rights Movement. Now Vine City, where she lived, was run down, boarded up, drugged out, and facing gentrification. Yet, her Victorian style home still looked just as beautiful as it did when it was built in the early 1930s. Her neighbors had an incongruous reverence for her home. Decades of rumors and superstition secured its safety.

"She came to me in a dream. She told me to find you," the woman cried.

"Well, whatcha standing out there for? Come on in," Delilah said as she stepped to the side and allowed the young woman to pass. "What's your name chile?"

"Ruthie. Ruthie Miller," she replied.

Delilah closed the door behind them and escorted Ruthie into the living room. Plastic covered the furniture and a picture of black Jesus, Martin Luther King, Malcom X, and Obama holding hands hung over the love seat.

"Sit down. I'll be back," Delilah directed as she disappeared from the room and reappeared with a cold glass of lemonade and a plate of cookies. "Here," she handed it to Ruthie and sat down beside her.

Ruthie took a bite and washed it down with lemonade that was so sweet she felt electricity shoot through her veins. She shook off the sugar rush and placed the snack and drink upon the marble top coffee table.

"What did you dream? What did Johnnie say?" Delilah inquired. She placed her hand on the trembling woman's knee, instantly calming her.

"I dreamed that I was being chased by a giant two headed snake," answered Ruthie.

"That's your past and your present chasing you honey. What color was it?" asked Delilah. "The color tells it all."

"Black," answered Ruthie. "It was big, black and scary!"

"That's danger chile! Someone in your life is definitely trying to do you in. What happened next?" asked Delilah with a look of recognition in her eyes. She shook her head slowly and twisted her lips.

"The snake was on my tail when this woman stepped in front of it and blocked its path. I recognized her as great grandma Johnnie from the family photo albums. The snake began to bite her. Blood splattered everywhere. Before it swallowed her whole, she told me to find you because you can kill it."

"Snake bites mean that you're afraid of someone. Better yet, that she's afraid of someone because she was the one bitten. The part of the dream that throws me is that she was swallowed. That usually represents love or passion. What's going on?" Delilah asked.

"I think my boyfriend put a root on me," Ruthie whispered. "I broke up with him and he's angry."

"Why do you believe in such nonsense?" Delilah asked as she shook her head. "Nobody can't put nothing on you..."

Ruthie lifted her t-shirt and under the skin of her belly, it looked like a million snakes were crawling. They writhed under her flesh causing her stomach to move in deep folds. It looked like moving fried funnel cake batter.

"Hot damn!" Delilah bleated. "Imma need Samson for this. Who is the man you're running from?"

"His name is Franklin Smith," Ruthie answered.

Delilah frowned and asked, "Where is his people from?"

"From here in Atlanta. They live in Mechanicsville," Ruthie replied. "His grandfather..."

"I know who his grandfather is, who his great grandfather is, and who his great great grandfather is. Hell, I think I know who he is," Delilah replied with a crooked smile on her face. She looked deeply into Ruthie's eyes and said, "I can't believe you still playing this game."

"What do you mean?" Ruthie asked, confusion distorting her face.

Delilah got up and walked to a bookshelf in the corner of the room. She picked up an old photo album and knocked the dust off it. She sat back down next to Ruthie, opened the book, and flipped through the pages until she came to a photo of a beautiful young woman who looked shockingly like Ruthie and a tall, dark, and attractive man with a solemn look on his face.

"He look familiar?" Delilah asked as she rolled her eyes upward.

"He looks like my…"

"Like your boyfriend," Delilah finished Ruthie's sentence. "You fools have been playing this game for centuries," Delilah laughed.

"What are you talking about?" Ruthie asked bewildered and deeply frustrated. She instantly regretted darkening Delilah's doorstep. She felt like a fool.

The front door swung open and Samson shuffled in with a paper bag in his hand. He looked at the two women and said, "They had a sale on sage, so I bought you a bunch to make bundles. We need to cleanse the energy in this house. Ever since Charlie came here last week begging us to get rid of that haint in his house, the energy has been off in here. We gotta clean it before a haint try to set up in here!" He looked at Ruthie and said, "Hey Johnnie. Back so soon?" He shook his head and headed to the medicine room.

Delilah slapped her knee and started laughing.

"What's so funny?" Ruthie asked with a voice tinged with anger and perplexity.

"What's funny is that you and that conjure man of yours have loved and killed each other for at least six lifetimes and each time, you come looking for us to save you," Delilah answered. "When will you figure out he ain't good for you chile?"

"That's ridiculous!" Ruthie snapped. She had always heard rumors of Samson and Delilah being old, but she refused to believe that they were that old. That would make them immortal.

"Just as ridiculous as those snakes wiggling around in yo' belly?" Delilah rebutted. "How did he get them in there this time? Did you swallow some candy during a kiss, or did he convince you to let him put his man cream on your belly while whispering a little prayer?"

"Can you help me or no?" Ruthie asked, irritated by the old woman's accusations. Just a day ago Franklin and Ruthie made love on a blanket in Grant Park. Although she refused to take him back, she couldn't refuse one last roll in the hay, so she allowed him to bless her belly with his lotion. She thought his prayer was for their reconciliation, but now she knew it was nothing more than a vengeful spell. Now her stomach was crawling with serpents that felt like they were eating her from the inside out.

"I can help you. I always do." Delilah sighed. "Come on gal. Follow me."

The young woman got up and followed Delilah into her healing room. Samson stood in the corner grinding something with a mortar and pestle and poured the powder into a crystal glass. He poured a dark liquid over the powder and a bubbling hiss filled the room.

"Drink this," he said and gave the glass to Ruthie. She drank the potion. Delilah instructed Ruthie to lie down and she obediently obliged.

The couple placed their hands on Ruthie's stomach and begin to sing. Their melodious voices filled the room with such beauty and power that Ruthie began to cry. They called up their ancestors and asked God for the power and permission to heal. Their hands became hot against Delilah's skin, so hot that she began to flinch. Samson and Delilah cried out and lifted their hands into the air. A thin line appeared across Ruthie's stomach. Small droplets of blood pushed through the miraculous incision. The opening widened and snake heads poked through her belly. The serpents danced upward like they were being bewitched by a snake charmer. The tips of their noses were drawn to the palms of the elderly couple like magnets. They kept singing until the last serpent exited Ruthie's stomach. When they stopped singing, the snakes hit the floor and slithered off into a dark corner. Samson went to gather them and throw them into the backyard as Delilah placed her hands on Ruthie's belly and prayed until the gaping hole in her stomach was nothing more than a gross memory.

"Get up chile," Delilah said as she stepped back to give room.

Ruthie sat up, befuddled by what had occurred. She didn't know whether to laugh or cry, so she just threw her arms around Delilah and said thank you.

"You're welcome baby," Delilah laughed.

Samson came shuffling back into the room cussing about how he was too old to be catching snakes and how he was tired of dealing with Johnnie and Frank's foolery every other century.

Ruthie walked over to hug Samson, but he stopped her and told her it wasn't necessary.

"Thank you anyway," Ruthie said.

"Let me walk you to the door," Delilah offered holding her lower back and walking like her feet hurt.

"No worries. I remember the way out. Thanks again," Ruthie waved and made her way to the front door.

Samson waved her away and grumbled, "See you next lifetime."

SCHOOL BUS STOP

He peered through the blinds every day at 3 p.m., watching the little brown boy get off the school bus. A bead of sweat formed on the middle-aged man's pink forehead every time he saw the beautiful brown boy sprint down the green hill after school. A crooked smile would expose the pink man's yellow teeth as he rubbed his gnarled hands together and fought to control the quickening of his breath. The man dreamed of the day when the boy would be alone, but somehow every day out of nowhere a tall dark man appeared when the school bus pulled up to the corner of the street. The dark man waited at the bus stop for the boy every day and walked him home. Sometimes the dark figure would look towards the pink man's window as if he knew what foul creature was lurking behind the bent dusty blinds.

One late spring afternoon, the little brown boy and his friends decided to knock on every door in their neighborhood so they could sell chocolate bars for their park basketball team. Two of the boys who accompanied him were called into the house early, and the little brown boy was left alone to sell the last five candy bars. Instead of giving up and going home, the little brown boy walked to the old gray house that no one ever visited and knocked on the door. With a loud creak, the door swung open and the pink man stood in the doorway wearing charcoal coveralls and his gritty yellow smile.

"Hello mister," the boy said as his eyes ran across the old man's face. There was something about the pink man's translucent eyes that reminded the little brown boy of every scary movie he had ever seen. Suddenly a chill ran up the boy's small arm. His chest tightened. He began to search his pockets; he had left his inhaler at home.

"Would you like to buy some candy to help support my basketball team?" he wheezed. His asthma hadn't bothered him in a very long time; he didn't understand why it had chosen to bother him that day.

The old man's eyes glistened as he licked his chapped lips. His heart leapt within his chest. Today was the day that his wildest dreams were going to come true.

"Sure," the pink man said. "Step inside while I get my wallet."

Apprehensively, the brown boy stepped inside the door. He knew he shouldn't have. His parent's voices telling him to be wary of strangers echoed through his head.

The house was dim and smelled like a dead squirrel the boy once found in the woods behind his house. It smelled so bad that he could taste the odor. Vomit bubbled in the back of his throat but was instantly swallowed down. A barking dog could be heard behind a door, and a strange whimper could be heard behind another. The brown boy turned to go back outside when the pink man suddenly reappeared and grabbed his arm and growled, "Not so fast! Where are you going?"

"I think I hear my mommy calling me," the brown boy lied. Tears started to run down his eyes. "Let me go; you're hurting my arm."

The pink man pulled the screaming boy down the hall, threw him into a room and slammed the door. A twin bed sat in the corner of the room. Something was rustling under it.

"I'll be back," the pink man said; his yellow teeth glistening behind a sinister grin. He left the room.

The brown boy cried hysterically. The rustling beneath the bed became louder. Curiosity outweighed his desire to wail. Yelping dissolved into sniffles as he looked under the bed and was met by two glossy green eyes. An ashen girl with greasy orange hair and a dirt-smeared face quivered beneath the old wooden bedframe.

"Where did you come from?" the brown boy asked.

"He grabbed me when I got off the bus yesterday," she whispered. "My mommy can't find me." Her stomach growled louder than her voice.

"Are you hurt?" the boy asked as he pointed to the blood on her dress.

The girl shook her head no. The blood was from her nose. It bled every time she was nervous. It had bled a lot since she had been abducted.

The brown boy reached out and gently pulled her from beneath the bed. Her clothes were torn and specked with red. Dust and lint stuck to her face. Dried blood flaked beneath her nose.

The brown boy began to weep. He was not old enough to understand what was going to happen, but he was old enough to understand fear; to understand that there was something evil in the eyes of the pink man and something horrible would happen to him and the ashen girl. He closed his eyes and grabbed the green-eyed girl's hand and cried, "God help us!"

The pink man reentered the room with a burlap bag and a video camera in his hand. A big knife was hanging from his belt and towels were draped over his shoulder. A wicked grin distorted his face as he reached for the boy. Before pink could meet brown, a dark hand grabbed hold of the pink man's arm and twisted. The sound of popping bones filled the room.

"Run!" the dark figure said without speaking. Somehow the boy heard it loud and clear. He grabbed the girl and the children hightailed out of the house, hand in trembling hand. A nearby neighbor saw them running hysterically and called the police and the children's parents.

Within minutes, the children were reunited with their parents and the police were dragging the pink man out of his house in handcuffs.

The pink man howled and screamed as his twisted arm folded oddly behind his back; white bones breaking through engorged flesh and bloody cloth grossed the children out. No one acknowledged his cries as he was pushed into the backseat of the car.

"What happened?" the beige officer asked the brown boy and orange-haired girl.

"I was selling candy and he asked me to step inside so he can get his money. I felt a little funny because his house was so creepy. I was gonna leave, but he grabbed me and threw me in the room with her. He was going to get us; then, the other man came and saved us," the brown boy replied.

"What other man?" the police officer asked. He instructed the other officers to check the house.

"The man who walks me home from the bus stop every day after school," the brown boy answered holding on tight to his mother's leg.

"You never told me about anyone walking you home?" the brown boy's father said, his face twisted, and brows furrowed.

The orange-haired girl lifted her head from the nape of her father's neck with a confused look on her face. He shifted her to his other hip so she could face the questioning officer.

She responded, "I didn't see another man."

"He was there," the brown boy exclaimed. "He was standing between us and the bad man."

"All I saw was the bad man yelling about his arm after I heard a loud pop. He fell to the floor; then we ran!" she cried.

The police and the parents looked at each other. The other officers exited the house informing the beige officer that the house was clear.

"He was there. He saved us!" the brown boy exclaimed; his father patted him on the head as a sign of belief.

The police officer said, "Whatever happened here, I'm glad you're both okay. The FBI has been looking for this reprobate for over ten years. He has done a lot of evil things and a lot of young lives have been lost. Whoever the mystery man was or wasn't, we all should thank God the children are safe."

The parents thanked the officers and headed back to their homes. The little brown boy unwrapped his arms from his mother's leg before his father grabbed him and put him on his back.

As they walked into their house, the boy looked across the yard and smiled.

The dark man smiled back and ascended into the sky in a wisp of smoke.

SERKET

Her eyes opened; shapes shifted and took form. Air was sucked into her lungs. Her chest expanded with sacred breath, and her spirit stirred within her. Space and time paused then resumed as she blinked. Tears rimmed her chestnut brown eyes that shined wide and full of knowing. Scarlet goo glistened from her pitch-black skin as she screamed to the top of her lungs.

"One more push!" the midwife instructed as she sat between legs trembling in pain. She cupped her hand to catch the life that was crowning before her eyes. Hair pushed from the womb, then a head, then a beautiful body perfect in every way.

"It's a girl," the midwife exclaimed as she held the tiny child above her head and thanked the great God for the new life in her hands. "Blessed be!" she shouted in exaltation and handed the baby to her mother. Kemet had birthed a new generation.

Queen Pebatjma, charcoal legs still spread wide and body soaked in sweat, kissed her daughter's gooey head and passed her back to Tuya, the midwife, to be cleaned. The queen fell back on her pillows and breathed easy for what felt like the first time in eons.

Queen Pebatjma had been in labor for sixteen hours. She timed it by Pharaoh Kashta's appearance every two hours. His intense anticipation seemed to make Pebatjma's contractions more forceful as if the child ached to see its father as much as he ached to see it. It had been an hour since he had last appeared with impatient eyes searching for a new development. Time rested deep into the night. By now, the queen was almost positive that her husband was resting his head on his couch, dreaming of holding his newborn son or daughter.

The old woman cleansed the baby in a basin of fresh water sprinkled with spices. She wrapped the baby in swaddling clothes, heaped blessings upon her head, fastened a charm around the child's wrist, and took her back to her mother.

"What will she be called?" Tuya asked, a smile on her dark leathery face. Deep wrinkles creased the sides of her eyes and the corners of her thick lips. She was pretty for someone so ancient. Youthful eyes and a mouth full of sparkling white teeth solidified her beauty. Her body was short and stout with burly arms and strong legs. Her hair was braided like an intricate basket, full of textures, twists and turns forming a floral-like crown.

It was rumored that Tuya had delivered the pharaoh's babies for the past thousand years. Her name had been written in the histories for ages and there was not a royal alive who, nor their grandparents, did not know her. It is said that Tuya came from the southern lands, where all humanity had begun, into Kemet when the gods walked the earth. Legend claimed that she saw the sands give birth to the pyramids and that she knew Ra before he became a god. She was rumored to have seen the waters being separated from the waters and her feet was one of the first to step onto dry land when it appeared. She was called Wisdom, wife of Knowledge.

It had been a long time since the gods had walked among the children of the earth. Only the pharaohs clung to divinity in a desperate attempt to control power, but Tuya remembered that there was a time when the gods truly walked the earth and her visions showed her that they would come back one day.

"I will call her Amenirdis," Queen Pebatjma answered while showering kisses upon her daughter's tiny head. "She is so beautiful."

"Indeed," agreed Tuya; nodding at the new mother and child with admiration in her eyes.

The baby was reddish brown like her father, Pharaoh Kashta, with a crown of wavy hair. Her face looked to be his as well, but it was much too early to tell; for babies morphed many times within the first year of their lives. It was almost a guarantee that she would grow up to be a striking beauty like her mother.

"Sweet child," the old lady cooed. "Indeed, blessed be."

The door swung open. Between two heavy muscled, topless guards, Tyti, a high-ranking house servant, walked into the room. She bowed to the queen and rolled her eyes at the old midwife.

"The child has come," Tyti stated with a look of chagrin. Her folded arms and disappointed eyes made Tuya cut her teeth.

"Shall I inform the king?" Tyti asked the queen, not removing her eyes from the wrinkly child in her arms.

"Let him sleep until I am fit for viewing," answered the queen. "I want him to see me at my best."

Blood and afterbirth soaked the linens beneath her and the marble floor surrounding her birthing bed. Soiled towels were scattered everywhere like dragonwort. Queen Pebatjma's bald head shined with perspiration; her braided wig sat on a nearby table spread out like a sleeping spider.

Tyti turned her nose up and let out a sigh of disgust as her eyes scrutinized the ebony queen and her clay colored baby.

Tuya's face twisted in anger as Tyti eyed the queen and her child. It was unfathomable why Tyti was not put out of the palace years ago. Spying was the girls second nature. Her devious green eyes seemed to be peaking around every corner, and miraculously moments after, the pharaoh would be told an altered version of what Tyti claimed to have witnessed. It was said that she was a worshipper of Set and she embodied a magic that was so diabolical that it would make even Anubis fear death. Tuya believed that maybe it was the girl's magic that held the pharaoh in her favor. That seemed like the only logical explanation that would keep the girl in the royal home. At first Tuya thought that the pharaoh fancied the girl, but there was no indication of an affair. He was truly smitten by his queen.

"May I clean up?" Tyti asked, her honey brown face wrecked with jealousy. It was no secret that she was in love with the pharaoh. She swooned at the sound of his voice and showered him with praises at every chance. Every night she envisioned herself in his arms instead of his wife. Tyti hated that her seductive advances were either thoroughly ignored by the king and that he was completely oblivious to any other woman but his wife. Tyti found the pharaoh's fawning over his wife utterly pathetic. Every inch of Tyti was annoyed with the queens overly joyous and helpful disposition. It seemed like nothing ever got under the queen's skin. Yet, it was clear that Pebatjma only tolerated Tyti because her family had served the crown for generations. Tyti used her families' legacy to her advantage and manipulated every situation to her benefit.

Tuya had warned Pebatjma time and time again about the dangers of Tyti, but the queen would not get rid of the girl. Tradition and loyalty were everything to the queen; so, until Tyti was caught in wrongdoing, she would continue to serve.

"Yes, you may clean up," Queen Pebatjma answered, handing the baby to Tuya.

Tuya sat in the corner of the room with the baby pressed to her bosom in quiet observation.

Tyti pulled the basin filled with crimson colored water out of the room and returned with fresh water for the new mother to wash. A group of women came in to clean the chamber as Tyti helped the queen bathe. The smell of soap and perfume overtook the scent of birth and blood. Within an hour, the queen was dressed in a fresh tunic, gold cuffs glistened on her wrists, a hand carved choker embraced her neck, and bird shaped earrings dangled from her ears. She looked like an onyx goddess perfectly carved by the gods. The once blood splattered chamber now looked pristine, and the cleaning women left as quick as they had come.

Amenirdis began to cry.

"Time to nurse," Tuya said as she stood up.

Tyti rushed over to the old woman and said," Let me take the princess to the queen."

Tuya looked at Pebatjma and she nodded her permission for the baby to be handed to Tyti. Tyti roughly pulled the infant from the old woman's arms and sauntered over to the queen. The queen reached out her arms and the servant dropped the baby into them.

"Be careful!" the queen hissed. "Watch how you handle my child!"

"Clumsy me," Tyti mumbled, and rolled her eyes.

"It's time for you to leave," Tuya barked, her strong legs crossing the room in mammoth strides.

"You are not my authority," Tyti barked, her young face sneering and ready for attack.

The baby began to scream.

"Get out of here," the queen ordered; sweat bubbling on her forehead. "Guards!" the queen called.

Silence.

"Your guards are loyal to me! Never underestimate my womanly talents," Tyti guffawed with arms folded and head thrown back.

The queen and Tuya eyes met in panic. It was too much of a fragile time for battle.

"The pharaoh ordered me to bring him the child," Tyti lied; reaching out for the baby.

The queen slapped Tyti's hands away.

"Over my dead body!" the queen hissed, clenching the baby to her chest. "Your time here has come to an end. Out of respect for your ancestors, I have tolerated you. Leave this palace at once or I will gift you with your own head!"

Admonition gleamed in the queen's eyes. If forced, she would gladly be a death dealer; for her delicate hands were full of strength and skillful danger.

"So be it! The pharaoh will be sickened by the loss of you and the child, but I will help him through his grief. I will offer him comfort like he has never known. What a spectacle the royal mourners will make over your cold dead body," Tyti seethed in anger as she pulled a vile from the top of her tunic, removed the lid, then tossed its contents at the queen. The dark, smelly liquid hit the queen's arm with a loud sizzle. She began to howl like her soul was being ripped from her flesh. A sprinkle of the poison hit the baby's lip and the child lapped it up like her mother's milk.

"No," Tuya screamed as she pushed Tyti to the floor a moment too late. Tuya rushed to the queen's side and frantically began to pray and chant seemingly worthless incantations over her wounds.

Queen Pebatjma screamed, writhing in pain, her flesh bubbled like hot tar.

The child latched onto her mother's arm, like a breast, and sucked the poison out in frantic gulps. Tuya tried to pull the baby away, but the child was unmovable. Soon, Pebatjma's cries faded from a horrific wail to a faint whimper into a painless sniffle. She looked down at her daughter, dazed and confused. Queen Pebatjma's arm was completely healed, and Amenirdis' countenance became more beautiful and vibrant than before. Her small features seemed to mature into a child half a year older.

Amenirdis turned towards the vicious servant and Tyti's smile was ripped from her face.

"Death!" the young woman squealed as she stepped backwards; her wide feet slapping the marble floor like drums.

The child pointed her tiny newborn finger at Tyti and a swarm of scorpions appeared out of the floor and surrounded her feet. The gold bangles on her wrists and arms morphed into serpents who sank their dripping fangs into the golden flesh of her arms and neck.

"Serket!" Tuya screamed as the scorpion's tails struck Tyti's feet over and over until they were two bubbling mounds of flesh. The young woman fell to the floor foaming at the mouth; her skin a putrid green and blistering in wet goo. Tyti's vacant eyes rolled backwards and she was gone.

"The goddess has returned!" Queen Pebatjma whispered as she held her baby at arm's length and looked into her omniscient eyes. The queen pulled the child back to her bosom and waited for her king to come.

Tuya fell prostrate before the child; singing hymns of praise to Serket, with tears of joy.

Little Amenirdis smiled and turned to her befuddled mother's breast and latched on.

WEDDING DAY KARMA

It was raining when I awoke. I can't believe today is the day that I am getting married. I've been dreaming about this day for the last two years, and it's finally happening; maybe not to my dream guy, but to a nice guy. Andreus is the salt of the earth. I've never known anyone so kind. He's not the most handsome man in the world, and he's definitely not the smartest; but he is a business guru, and a serious money magnet. His friends hate me. They think I'm a gold digger, but that's not true. I just like nice things. I really do like him. I've never liked anyone so much. A matter of fact, I think I like him so much that one day, if I try really hard, I think I can grow to love him.

His friends think that he should marry his best friend and college sweetheart Latrice. She's a nice girl, but she doesn't look half as good as I do. I felt that he could do better. It was way too easy for me to take him from her. I simply photoshopped a picture of her kissing another guy. He was so hurt that he broke up with her instantly; and I was there to pick up the pieces. He found out that the photo was fake, but he still doesn't know I was behind it. He apologized to Latrice and she forgave him; but Andreus and I were together, so they decided to be friends. A year ago, he asked me to marry him. I knew then that she was truly out of his system.

If I hurry into the shower, I'll be able to get to the church before everyone else. I like to walk around the peaceful old building. There is something truly spiritual, for lack of a better word, in the silence of its architecture. That's tremendous for me since I'm an atheist.

I'm so happy Andreus installed new shower heads. The water feels heavenly. Where's my shampoo? Oh, here it is. A quick lather and…. Ouch! My eyes! The water isn't rinsing fast enough. I drop the shampoo bottle. I blindly search for it, but I knock over the soap and my bath oil. I try to stand but my feet won't stop sliding. I fall into the shower glass. Ouch! My head! Blood everywhere! I rinse the blood down the drain. I check the mirror to make sure my face is still perfect. Flawless! I towel off. It would have been awful for me to have shown up looking like I had a fight with a honey badger.

I quickly get dressed. I'm so happy that my bridesmaids have my dress and accessories. All I have to do is get there. I decide to walk to the church since it's only four blocks away. I have plenty of time to spare, might as well enjoy the spring breeze.

Oh no! Am I late? Why are so many people at the church already? I look at the big clock on the local bank tower and it says 4:45pm. How can this be? My wedding was supposed to start at two! How can I possibly be so late? I go inside of the church and peek in the door of the sanctuary. The wedding party and guests are clearly upset, so I run to the back and quickly get dressed. I make my way down the church isle and stand in front of an angry Andreus. Someone whispers something in his ear. He weeps. I tell him not to cry; that I'm sorry I'm late; I'm here now; and that we can start the ceremony. He ignores me and walks out of the church. I follow him and jump in the passenger side of the car. His friends Latrice and Saadiq follow behind us. Andreus speeds home. Our driveway is filled with emergency vehicles. He runs inside, and I am on his heels. An officer tells Andreus to follow him. My mother is standing in my bathroom wailing. Andreus and I enter the bathroom and we see *me* lying on the floor of the shower with a large piece of glass sticking out of my head. I try to run to my body, but a blinding light engulfs me. The last thing I saw before the world went white was Latrice wrapping her arms around Andreus.

Questions for Book Clubs

1. What are some of the reoccurring themes in the stories?
2. Which was your favorite story? Why?
3. Which is your least favorite story? Why?
4. Were you familiar with all the creatures in this book?
5. Who was the most likable/dislikable character(s)? Why?
6. How did the stories make you feel?
7. Were the plots engaging? Does it unfold slowly or is it a fast page turner?
8. If you could ask the author a question, what would you ask?
9. Did you learn anything new?
10. Were the stories predictable?

Violette L. Meier is a happily married mother, writer, folk artist, poet, inspirational leader and native of Atlanta, Georgia, who earned her B.A. in English at Clark Atlanta University and a Master of Divinity at Interdenominational Theological Center.

The great-granddaughter of a dream interpreter, Violette is a lover of all things supernatural and enjoys writing paranormal, fantasy, and horror among other speculative fiction genres. She is the author of twelve books and is always working on something new.

To learn more about Violette, please visit her at www.violettemeier.com.